BRIDE TO THE KING

BRIDE TO THE KING

BARBARA CARTLAND

Thorndike Press • Chivers Press
Waterville, Maine USA   Bath, England

This Large Print edition is published by Thorndike Press, USA and by Chivers Press, England.

Published in 2002 in the U.S. by arrangement with International Book Marketing Limited.

Published in 2002 in the U.K. by arrangement with Cartland Promotions.

U.S. Hardcover 0-7862-3628-0   (Candlelight Series Edition)
U.K. Hardcover 0-7540-4790-3   (Chivers Large Print)
U.K. Softcover 0-7540-4791-1   (Camden Large Print)

The text of this Large Print edition is unabridged.
Other aspects of the book may vary from the original edition.

Set in 16 pt. Plantin by Rick Gundberg.

Printed in the United States on permanent paper.

British Library Cataloguing in Publication Data available

Library of Congress Cataloging-in-Publication Data

Cartland, Barbara, 1902–
  Bride to the king / Barbara Cartland.
    p. cm.
  ISBN 0-7862-3628-0 (lg. print : hc : alk. paper)
  1. Large type books. I. Title.
PR6005.A765 B75 2002
823´.912—dc21   2001036778

Author's Note

During the Franco-Prussian War in 1870 negotiations were pushed ahead for the unity of all Germany outside Austria. A conference of Prussia, Bavaria, and Würtemberg met at Munich to discuss the terms of unification. There was the question of the name for the new State, and Bismarck wished to revive the title of Emperor. On January 18, 1871, King Wilhelm Freidrich I was proclaimed Emperor, in the Galerie des Glaces at Versailles.

The new Reich consisted of four Kingdoms, five Grand Duchies, thirteen Duchies and Principalities, and three free cities.

The rest of Europe was appalled and frightened.

Chapter One

1875

"Zosina, wake up!"

The girl addressed started and raised her eyes from the book she had been reading.

"Did you speak to me?" she asked.

"For the third time!" her sister Helsa replied.

"I am sorry. I was reading."

"That is nothing new," Helsa exclaimed. "*Fraulein* says that you will ruin your eyes and be blind before you are middle-aged."

Zosina laughed a soft, musical laugh with an undoubted note of amusement in it.

"Although it is *Fraulein*'s job to teach us," she said, "she always finds marvellous excuses for us not to learn anything."

"Of course she does," Theone remarked, who was painting one of the fashion magazines with watercolours. "*Fraulein* knows so little herself, she is afraid that if we show any intelligence we will realise how little she can tell us."

"I feel that is rather unkind," Zosina said.

7

"Kind or not," Helsa replied, "if you do not hurry downstairs, since Papa wants you, you will be in trouble."

"Papa wants me?" Zosina said in surprise. "Why did you not tell me so?"

"That is just what I have been trying to do," Helsa replied. "Margit came in just now to say Papa wanted you in his Study. You know what that means!"

Zosina gave a little sigh.

"I suppose I must have forgotten something he told me to do, but I cannot think what it is."

"You will learn quickly enough," Theone remarked. "I am thankful it is not me he has sent for."

Zosina rose from the window-seat on which she had been sitting and walked across the School-Room to look in the mirror over the mantelshelf.

She tidied her hair, quite unaware that her reflection portrayed a lovely face with large grey eyes which at the moment were rather worried.

She was in fact concentrating fiercely on trying to remember something she had done wrong or something she had omitted to do.

Whatever it was, she was quite certain her father would make it an opportunity to be extremely disagreeable, a thing at which he excelled these days, when he was suffering from gout.

Without saying more to her sisters, Zosina crossed the room to leave, and as she did so, Katalin, who had not spoken until now and who was only twelve, looked up to say:

"Good luck, Zosina. I wish I could come with you."

"That would only make Papa more angry than he is already," Zosina said with a smile.

Leaving the School-Room, she hurried down the long passages, which were extremely cold in the winter, until she reached the front staircase of the Palace.

The Arch-Duke Ferdinand of Lützelstein lived in considerable style, which impressed the more distinguished of his subjects but was criticised by those who suspected that they had to pay for it.

But he did not give his family much comfort or consideration, and they knew it was because they had committed the unforgivable sin of being daughters instead of sons.

There was no doubt that the Arch-Duke was bitterly disappointed and frustrated by the fact that he had no direct heir.

"You are his favourite," Katalin would often say irrepressibly to Zosina, "because you were his first disappointment. Helsa was Number Two and Theone was Number

Three. By the time he reached me, he disliked me so much I am only surprised he did not cut me up into small pieces and scatter me from the battlements!"

Katalin had a dramatic imagination and, perhaps because she lacked the affection of her father and her mother, was always thinking herself wildly in love with one of the younger officials in the Palace or, more understandably, the Officers of the Guard.

Zosina was in many ways very different from her sisters.

They had a practical and sensible outlook on life which made them accept the family difficulties, and the small but tiresome privations to which they were subject, as an inevitable quirk of fate.

"If I had the choice, I would rather have been born the daughter of a forester," Theone had said once, "than a Royal Princess without any of the glamour or excitement that should go with it."

"You will get that when you are grown up," Zosina had answered.

Theone had laughed.

"What about you? You were allowed to go to your 'Coming Out' Ball, but you had to dance with all the oldest and more boring officials in the country. Since then Mama has made no effort to entertain for you, unless you call it being entertained when you are allowed to sit in the Drawing-Room when she receives the Councillors' wives and they talk about their charities or something equally deadly!"

Zosina had to admit that these were not particularly exciting occasions.

At the same time, she had learnt long ago not to be bored with having to listen to the stiff, desultory conversation which was all that the Palace etiquette permitted.

"The weather has been cold lately," her mother would say, starting the conversation as protocol directed.

"It has indeed, Your Royal Highness."

"I often say to the Arch-Duke that the winds at this time of year are very treacherous."

"They are indeed, Your Royal Highness."

"We will all be thankful when the warm weather comes."

"It is something we all look forward to, Your Royal Highness."

Zosina was not listening. Her thoughts had carried her far away into a fantasy-world where people talked intelligently and wittily.

Or else she was on Mount Olympus, mixing with gods and goddesses of Ancient Greece and pondering on the problems to which mankind had tried through all eternity to find a solution.

The Arch-Duchess would have been astounded if she had known how knowledgeable her eldest daughter was on the behaviour, a great deal of it outrageous, of the Greek gods.

She would have been equally astonished if she had known that Zosina pored over books written by French authors which gave an insight into the strange diversions that had invaded French literature during the Second Empire.

Zosina was fortunate in that the Palace Library, which had been started by her great-grandfather, was considered one of the treasures of Lützelstein.

It therefore behoved the present Ruler, Arch-Duke Ferdinand, to keep it up, for which fortunately an endowment from Parliament was provided every year.

New books were purchased and added to the thousands already accumulated, and the Librarian, an elderly man, was easily persuaded by Princess Zosina to put on his list of requirements those books which she particularly wanted to read.

"I am not sure that Her Royal Highness would approve," he would say occasionally when Zosina had pleaded for some author whose somewhat doubtful reputation had reached even Lützelstein.

"You are quite safe, *Mein Herr*," Zosina would say. "Mama never has time to read and so she is unlikely to criticise anything you have on your shelves."

She smiled as she spoke, and the Librarian had found himself smiling back and agreeing to anything which this extremely pretty girl demanded of him.

Zosina now reached the Hall and hurried to the door which led into her father's Study.

It was an extremely impressive room, the walls covered with dark panelling, the windows draped with heavily fringed velvet curtains, the furniture ponderous and old-fashioned.

It was a room which all four Princesses disliked intensely because it was always here that their father lectured them on their misdeeds and where they waited apprehensively for the moment when he would fly into one of his rages which usually ended in his storming at them:

"Get out of my sight! I have seen enough of all four of you! God knows why I should be inflicted with such stupid, fractious females instead of being blessed with an intelligent son!"

It was the signal for them to leave, but even though they found the relief of doing so almost inexpressible, their hearts would be

13

thumping and their lips dry.

In some way which they could not explain even to one another, they did not feel safe until they were back in the School-Room.

"What can I have done to upset Papa?" Zosina asked herself now.

Then with an instinctive little lift of her chin she opened the door and went in.

Her father was sitting, as she expected, in his favourite high-back winged arm-chair near the hearth.

There was no fire because it was summer, and it was typical, Zosina often thought, that in this room there was no arrangement of flowers to fill the empty fireplace, so that its gaping black mouth added to the general gloom.

The Arch-Duke had his gouty left leg, swathed in bandages, resting on a footstool in front of him, and Zosina thought with a little jerk of her heart that he was looking stern and grim.

She walked towards him, still wondering frantically what could be wrong, when to her surprise as she reached his side, he looked up at her and smiled.

The Arch-Duke had in his youth been an extremely handsome man, and it was therefore not surprising that his four daughters were all exceptionally good-looking.

14

Zosina had long ago decided that their features came in fact from their great-grandmother who had been Greek, and some of their other characteristics from their father's mother, who was Hungarian by birth.

"We are a mixture of nationalities," she had said once, "but we have been clever enough to take the best from every country whose blood is mixed with ours."

"If we had been really clever, we would not have been born in Lützelstein," Katalin had said irrepressibly.

"Why not?" Helsa had enquired.

"Well, if we had had the choice, surely we would have chosen France, Italy, or England."

"I see what you mean!" Helsa had exclaimed. "Well, I would have chosen France. I have heard how gay it is in Paris."

"Our Ambassador told Papa their extravagance and outrageous behaviour during the Second Empire was the scandal of the world."

"That is over now!" Theone had said. "But I bet the French still have a lot of fun. We should have been born in France!"

"Sit down, Zosina. I want to talk to you," the Arch-Duke said now.

Zosina obediently seated herself on the sofa near him, and he looked at her until she won-

15

dered if he disapproved of her gown or perhaps the new way in which she had arranged her hair.

Then he said:

"I have something to tell you, Zosina, that may surprise you. At the same time, at your age you must have been expecting it."

"What is that, Papa?"

"You are to be married!"

For a moment Zosina thought she could not have heard correctly.

Then as her eyes widened until they seemed to fill the whole of her small face, the Arch-Duke said:

"It is gratifying, very gratifying, that the negotiations of our Ambassador, Count Csáky, should prove so fruitful. I shall of course reward him in the proper manner."

"Are you . . . saying, Papa . . . that the Count has . . . arranged my . . . marriage?"

"At my instigation, of course," the Arch-Duke said. "But if I am truthful, I must admit that the first suggestion of such an alliance came from the Regent of Dórsia."

Zosina looked puzzled, and, as if her father understood, he said impressively:

"You, my dear, are to marry King Gyórgy!"

Zosina gave a little gasp, then said:

"But . . . Papa, I have never . . . seen him, and why should he . . . want to . . . marry me?"

16

"That is what I intend to explain to you," the Arch-Duke said, "so listen attentively."

"I . . . am, Papa."

"You are aware, of course," the Arch-Duke began, "that I have been worried for some time about the growing power of the German Empire."

"Yes, Papa," Zosina murmured.

As it happened, her father had never discussed it with her, but Zosina remembered how five years ago everybody else in the Palace had talked of little else, when the outbreak of the Franco–Prussian War made the policy of the Minister-President of Prussia, Otto von Bismarck, seem to threaten their independence.

Prussia had long been preparing for that war, and Bismarck had cunningly manipulated the situation so that her enemy, France, was made the technical aggressor.

In July 1870, France had declared war on Prussia, Bavaria, and other South-German Kingdoms and small Principalities sided with Prussia.

The issue had never been in any doubt, and in January the following year, after a terrible siege of 131 days, starving Paris opened its gates to the enemy.

In the South, the small Kingdoms which had not been engaged in the war, like

Lützelstein and Dórsia, had hoped that their large neighbour, Bavaria, would protect them from Bismarck's ambitions.

However, King Ludwig of Bavaria, always unpredictable, had been ill and therefore was not strong enough to stand up against the pressure placed upon him by Prussia's representative.

All this flashed through Zosina's mind, and she was not surprised when her father said:

"At this particular moment in history, it is absolutely essential that Lützelstein and Dórsia should be independent and keep the balance of power in Europe."

He paused before he continued impressively:

"We have a weakened Austria on one side of us, a limp Bavaria on the other, and Germany growing stronger every day, ready to draw us into the iron net of an inflexible Empire."

"I understand, Papa," Zosina murmured.

"I do not expect you to understand anything of the sort!" the Arch-Duke said suddenly, in an irritated tone of voice. "But listen to what I am saying, because it is for this reason that a close alliance, sealed by marriage between the King of Dórsia and one of my daughters, would strengthen the hands of the politicians in both countries."

Zosina wanted to say again that she understood, but instead she merely nodded her head, and her father said:

"Well, speak up! Do you grasp what I am trying to tell you? By God, if I had a son he would see the position quickly enough!"

"I see the reason, Papa, for the marriage," Zosina said. "But I asked you if the King . . . really wished to marry me."

"Of course he wishes to marry you!" the Arch-Duke thundered. "He can understand the situation clearly enough because he is a man and a Royal Monarch at that!"

"I should have thought, Papa, that the King and I . . . should have . . . met before everything was . . . decided," Zosina said in her soft voice.

"Meet? Of course you will meet!" the Arch-Duke snapped. "That is exactly what I am going to tell you. If you would stop interrupting, Zosina, I would be able to get to the point."

"I am . . . sorry, Papa."

"Your marriage is arranged to take place as soon as possible, as a warning to Germany that we will not be interfered with," the Arch-Duke said. "And because we must do things in a proper manner, I have arranged that the Queen Mother should pay a State Visit to Dórsia and take you with her."

Zosina's face lit up.

19

"I am to go with Grandmama to Dórsia, Papa? That will be exciting!"

"I am sorry I cannot go myself," the Arch-Duke said. "Both your mother and I would prefer it, of course, but, as you see, the damned leg of mine makes it impossible."

He winced as he spoke, and Zosina asked quickly:

"Is it very painful, Papa?"

The Arch-Duke bit back a swear-word and instead said hastily:

"I have no wish to talk about it. What I was saying is that you will accompany your grandmother on a State Visit, at the end of which your engagement will be publicly announced."

Zosina was silent for a moment, then she said:

"Supposing . . . Papa, the King . . . dislikes me and I . . . dislike him? Would we still have to be . . . married?"

Her father glared at her before he answered:

"A more stupid, idiotic question I have seldom heard! What does it matter if you like or dislike each other? It is a political matter, as I have just explained if you had listened!"

"I did listen, Papa. At the same time . . . political or not, it is I who have to . . . marry the King."

"And think yourself extremely lucky to do so!" the Arch-Duke stormed. "Good God, I have four daughters to get off my hands one way or another. You cannot imagine that I am going to find available Kings for all of them!"

Zosina drew in her breath.

"I suppose . . . Papa, you would not . . . consider Helsa . . . going instead of . . . me? She is very . . . anxious to be . . . married, while I am quite . . . happy to stay here with . . . you and Mama."

Her question, spoken in a somewhat hesitating voice, brought the blood coursing into her father's face.

"How dare you argue with me!" he raged. "How dare you suggest you will not do as you are told! You ought to go down on your knees and thank God that you have a father who considers you to the extent of providing you with a throne, which is not something to be picked up every day of the week!"

His voice deepened with anger as he went on:

"You will do exactly what I tell you! You will go to Dórsia with your grandmother and you make yourself pleasant to the King — do you understand?"

"Yes, Papa . . . but . . ."

"I am not listening to any arguments or anything else you have to say," the Arch-

Duke roared. "It is typical that after all I have done for you, I find that I have been nurturing a viper in my bosom! You are ungrateful besides apparently being — half-witted!"

He coughed over the word, then continued:

"There is not a girl in the whole Duchy who would not jump at such an opportunity, but not you! Oh no! You have to complain and find fault! God Almighty! Who do you expect will ask to marry you — the Archangel Gabriel?"

The Arch-Duke was really carried away in one of his rages by now, and Zosina, knowing that nothing she could say would abate the storm, rose to her feet.

"I am . . . sorry you are . . . angry, Papa," she said, "but thank you for . . . thinking of me."

She curtseyed and left the room while he shouted after her:

"Ungrateful and half-witted to boot! Why should I be afflicted with such children?"

Zosina shut the door and was glad as she went down the passage that she could no longer hear what he was saying.

"I should have kept silent," she told herself.

Her father had taken her by surprise and she knew that she had been extremely stupid to have questioned in any way one of his plans. It always annoyed him.

'He is also annoyed,' she thought, 'because he cannot make the State Visit himself. He would have enjoyed it so much. But it will be fun to go with Grandmama.'

Queen Szófia, the Queen Mother, was both admired and loved by her four grand-daughters.

Because she had an abundance of traditional Hungarian charm, she had captivated most of the population when she reigned in Lützelstein.

But there had been a hard core of Court Officials who found her frivolous and too free and easy in her ways.

Now, when she was well over sixty, she still appeared to laugh more than anyone else, and life in the small Palace to which she had retired, five miles away, always seemed to Zosina a place of happiness and gaiety.

She reached the Hall and was going towards the stairs when out of the shadows emerged Count Csáky, the Ambassador to Dórsia.

He was an elderly man whom Zosina had known all her life, and as soon as she realised that he wished to speak to her, she went towards him with her hand outstretched.

"How delightful to see you, Your Excellency!" she exclaimed. "I did not know you had returned home."

"I only returned two days ago, Your Royal Highness," he replied, bowing over her hand. "I imagine His Royal Highness has told you the news I brought him?"

"We have just been talking about it," Zosina replied, hoping that the Ambassador had not heard her father raging at her.

He smiled and said:

"In which case I have something to show you."

She walked with him into one of the Ante-Rooms where distinguished personages usually sat when they were awaiting an audience with her father.

The Count went to a table on which she saw a Diplomatic-Box. He opened it and drew out a small leather case.

He handed it to her and before she opened it she knew, without being told, that it contained a miniature of the King of Dórsia.

He was certainly good-looking, with dark hair and dark eyes.

He was wearing a white tunic resplendent with decorations and he appeared very impressive.

"I thought you would like to see it," the Ambassador murmured, standing beside her.

"It is very kind of Your Excellency," Zosina said. "I had been wondering what the King looked like, but actually, although I did not say so to Papa, I thought he was too young to marry."

"His Majesty comes of age in a month's time," the Count replied. "He will then be able to reign without the Regent, and the Prime Minister and the Privy Council consider it very important that when his uncle retires, he should have a wife to support him."

"His uncle has been the Regent for a long time?" Zosina asked, thinking it was expected of her.

"Yes, for eight years. The King was only twelve when his father died and his uncle was appointed Regent, and he has, I may say, ruled Dórsia on his nephew's behalf extremely well. It is a rich country, thanks to him. Your Royal Highness will have every comfort, besides living in what is to my mind one of the loveliest places in the world."

There was so much warmth in the Ambassador's voice that Zosina looked at him in surprise.

"I am not being disloyal, Your Royal Highness, to Lützelstein," the Count said quickly, "but as it happens, my mother came from Dórsia, and that is one of the reasons why I was so delighted to be appointed Ambassador there."

Zosina looked down at the miniature and said:

"I asked my father if the King . . . really wanted to marry me, but it . . . made him angry. I would like to . . . ask you the same . . . question."

She raised her eyes to the Count as she spoke, and he thought that any man would be only too willing and eager to marry anyone so lovely and so attractive in every way.

He had always thought Zosina was an exceptional girl and he was sure that with her intelligence, her beauty, and her inescapable charm, any country over which she reigned and any man whom she married would be extremely lucky.

Then as he realised that she was waiting for him to answer her question, he said:

"As it happens, Your Royal Highness, I took with me to Dórsia a miniature of yourself, since I thought the King would wish to see it as I have brought his portrait to you."

"And what did His Majesty say?" Zosina asked in a low voice.

"I do not know His Majesty's reaction," the Ambassador replied, "for the simple reason that my negotiations for the marriage took place with the Regent. I gave him the miniature so that there would be no mistake about it reaching His Majesty's own hands."

Zosina could not help feeling disappointed. She would have liked to know exactly what the King had said when he saw her portrait.

"I do understand," the Count said with a tact that was part of his profession, "that it is difficult for Your Royal Highness to contemplate marrying somebody you have never seen, even though you realise how expedient it is from the point of view both of Lützelstein and of Dórsia."

"I . . . accept that I have been born with a certain . . . state in life," Zosina said hesitatingly, "but at the same . . . time . . ."

She stopped because she knew she could not put into words — and if she did there was no point in it — that she did not want to be just a political pawn but something much more important to the man she would marry.

"Tell me about the King," she said, before the Ambassador could speak.

"He is, as you see, very handsome," the Count replied, and Zosina felt that he was choosing his words carefully. "He is young, but that is something which time will always remedy, and he enjoys life to the — full."

"In what way?"

She had a feeling that the Count would find this question rather hard to answer, and he hesitated quite obviously before he said:

"All young men find life exciting when they are first free of their Tutors and studies, and the King is no exception. But I think, Your

Royal Highness, it would be a mistake for me to say too much. I want you to judge for yourself and not go to Dórsia with a biased mind."

Zosina had the idea that the Ambassador was trying to get out of a rather difficult situation.

But why it should be difficult she was not certain.

She thought to herself shrewdly:

'He wants me to like the King and he is afraid that anything he might say would prejudice me one way or another.'

She looked down again at the miniature.

The King was good-looking, and almost as if she spoke to herself she said:

"He is . . . very young."

"Two years older than Your Royal Highness," the Ambassador replied, "and I am told by those who know him that he has old ideas in many ways, which is not surprising, seeing that he has been King for so many years."

"But it is the Regent who does all the work!" Zosina flashed.

"Not all of it," the Ambassador replied. "I think Prince Sándor has gone out of his way to see that the King fulfils a great number of official duties from which he might have been excused."

"Does His Majesty resent having a Regent to run the country for him?" Zosina asked.

"That is a question I cannot answer, Your Royal Highness. Knowing Prince Sándor as I do, I cannot imagine anybody resenting his authority, but one never knows with young people. I expect, however, that His Majesty will be very glad to be free of all restrictions except those of Parliament when he comes of age."

"He might find a . . . wife restricting too."

The Count smiled.

"That is something, Princess, which I feel you would never be to any man."

Zosina put the miniature down on the Diplomatic-Box.

"I thank Your Excellency very much for being so kind," she said. "You will be coming with me and the Queen Mother to Dórsia?"

There was almost an appeal in her voice, and the look she gave him told the Ambassador that she thought it would be a help and a comfort to have him there.

"I shall be with Your Royal Highness," he replied, "and you know I am always ready to be of assistance at any time and in any way that you require."

"Thank you," Zosina said simply.

She held out her hand, then without saying any more she left the Ante-Room and walked swiftly across the marble Hall and started to climb the stairs.

Only when she was halfway up them did

she begin to hurry, and ran along the corridors to burst into the School-Room.

As three faces turned to look anxiously at her, she realised that her breath was coming quickly between her lips and her heart was pounding in her breast.

"What is it? What has happened?" Helsa asked.

"Was Papa very disagreeable?" Theone questioned.

For a moment it was impossible for Zosina to answer. Then Katalin jumped up and ran to put her arms round her waist.

"You look upset, Zosina," she said sympathetically. "Never mind, dearest, we love you, and however beastly Papa may be, we will all try to make you feel better."

Zosina put her arm round Katalin's shoulders.

"I am . . . all right," she said in a voice which shook, "but I have had rather a . . . shock."

"A shock?" Helsa exclaimed. "What is it?"

"I do not . . . know how to . . . tell you."

"You must tell us," Katalin said. "We always share everything, even shocks."

"I cannot . . . share this."

"Why not?"

"Because I am to be . . . married."

"Married?"

Three voices shrieked the words in unison.

"It cannot be true!"

"As Papa has said so . . . I suppose it . . . will be!"

"Who are you to marry?" Theone enquired.

"King György of Dórsia!"

For a moment there was a stupefied silence. Then Katalin cried:

"You will be a Queen! Oh, Zosina, how marvellous! We can all come and stay with you and get away from here!"

"A Queen! Heavens, you are lucky!" Helsa exclaimed.

Zosina moved away to sit down on the window-seat where she had been reading before she went downstairs.

"I cannot . . . believe it," she said in a very small voice, "though it is true, because Papa said so. But it seems . . . strange and rather frightening to marry a man you have never . . . seen and know very little . . . about."

"I know a lot about him," Theone said.

Three faces looked at her.

"What do you mean? How can you know about him if we do not?"

"I heard Mama's Lady-in-Waiting talking to Countess Csáky when they did not know or had forgotten I was in the room."

"What did they say? Tell us what they said!" Helsa cried.

"The Countess said the King was wild and was always in trouble of some sort. Then she laughed and said: 'I often think the Arch-Duke is luckier than he knows in not having a son of that sort to cope with!' "

"How would she know that . . ." Helsa began, then interrupted herself to say: "Of course, the Countess is married to our Ambassador to Dórsia!"

"I have just been talking to him," Zosina said. "He showed me a miniature of the King."

"What does he look like? Tell us what he looks like!" her sisters cried.

"He is very handsome and did not look wild but rather serious."

"You would not be able to tell from a picture anyway," Theone said.

"If he is . . . wild," Zosina said slowly, "I expect that is why they want him to get . . . married . . . in case he causes a . . . scandal or . . . something."

She was really puzzling it out for herself when Katalin, who had followed her to the window-seat, sat down beside her and said:

"If he is like that, you will be a good influence on him. I expect that is why they want you to marry him."

"A . . . good influence?" Zosina faltered.

"Yes, of course! It is like all the stories: the

hero is a rake, he has a reputation with women, and he does all sorts of things of which people disapprove! Then along comes the lovely, good heroine and he finds his soul."

Helsa and Theone burst into laughter.

"Katalin, that is just like you to talk such nonsense!"

"It is not nonsense, it is true!" Katalin protested. "You mark my words, Zosina will reform the rake and make him into a good King, and she will end up by being canonised and having a statue erected to her in every Church in Dórsia!"

They all laughed again, Zosina with rather an effort.

"That is all a fairy-story," she said. "At the same time, I think I am . . . frightened of going to . . . Dórsia."

"Of course you are not!" Katalin said before anyone else could speak. "While you are there you will have a good time. I have often wondered what rakes do. Is there a word for a lady rake?"

"No," Helsa said. "Besides, while a man can be a rake, you know that a woman, if she did even half the things a man can do, would be condemned for being wicked, and no-one would speak to her."

"I suppose so," Katalin agreed, "and she would be thrown into utter darkness or dogs would eat her bones as happened to Jezebel."

Even Zosina laughed at this.

"In which case I think I would prefer to be canonised," she said. "But at the same time, I wish I could stay here. I did suggest to Papa that the King might prefer to marry Helsa."

Her sister gave a little cry.

"I would marry him tomorrow if I had the chance! For goodness' sake, Zosina, do not pretend you are reluctant to be a Queen! And if you grab the only King there is, and I have to put up with some poor minor Royalty, I shall die of sheer envy!"

"Perhaps when the King meets you when you go to Dórsia," Katalin said, "he will fall in love with you and will threaten to abdicate unless you will be his wife. Then everybody would be happy."

"It is quite a good story as it is," Helsa said. "Here we are sitting in the School-Room, going nowhere and meeting no men, unless you count those pompous old officials who come to see Papa, and suddenly Zosina is whisked off to be crowned Queen of Dórsia. It really is the most exciting thing that has happened for years!"

"Papa said I was . . . ungrateful, and I suppose I . . . am," Zosina said slowly. "It is just that I would like to have . . . fallen in love with the man I . . . marry."

There was silence for a moment. Then Theone said:

"I suppose we would all like that, but we have not much chance of it happening, have we?"

"Very little," Helsa said. "That is the penalty for being born Royal — to have to marry whom you are told to marry, with no argument about it."

Katalin put her head on one side.

"Perhaps that is why Papa is so disagreeable — because he did not want to marry Mama and always found her a bore."

"Katalin! How could you say such things?" Helsa asked.

"I do not know why you should be so shocked," Katalin answered. "You know how good-looking Papa was when he was young. I am sure he could have married anyone — Queen Victoria herself if he had wished to."

"He would have been too young for her," said Helsa, who was always the practical one.

"Well — anyone else with whom he fell in love."

"Perhaps he did," Katalin said. "Perhaps he was in love with a beautiful girl who was not Royal, and although they loved each other passionately, Papa was forced by his tiresome old Councillors to marry Mama."

"I am sure we should not be talking like

35

this," Zosina said, "and it does not make it any easier for me."

"I am being selfish and unkind," Katalin said hastily, "and we do understand what you are feeling — do we not, girls?"

"Yes, of course we do," Helsa and Theone agreed.

"It has been a shock, but at least he is young and handsome," Theone went on. "You must remind yourself if ever he is difficult, that he might well have been old and hideous!"

Zosina gave a little sigh and looked out the window.

She was trying to tell herself that she should be grateful and that, as Theone had just said, things might have been much worse.

She knew that what was really troubling her was that she had always dreamt that one day she would fall in love and it would be very wonderful.

All the books she had read had, in one way or another, shown her how important love was in the life of a man and a woman.

She had started with the love the Greeks knew and how it permeated their thinking and their living and was to them the most important emotion both for gods and for man.

It was love, Zosina thought, that motivated great deeds, caused wars, inspired the finest masterpieces of art and music, and made men at times as great as the gods they worshipped.

She thought now that beneath her endeavours to improve herself, to stimulate her mind, to acquire all the knowledge that was possible, there had been a desire to make herself better than she was.

Secretly she believed that one day the man who would love her would want her to be different from every other woman he had ever known.

In retrospect it seemed almost a foolish ambition.

Yet it had been there; and it was difficult, in the quiet, conventional life they had lived in the School-Room, to remember that they were Royal and their futures must therefore be different from those of other girls of their age.

Although it had struck Zosina occasionally that her marriage might eventually be arranged, it had never for one moment crossed her mind it would be to somebody she had never even seen.

That it would be a *fait accompli* before she had time to think about it or discuss it, or have the chance of refusing the prospective husband if she really disliked him, had never occurred to her.

"I have been very stupid," she told herself, but she knew that even if she had been anything else, the result would of course have been just the same.

It was only that deep in her heart something cried out at being pressurised and constrained into a situation in which she could only accept the inevitable and have no choice one way or the other.

'I suppose if it is too terrible . . . too frightening,' she thought, 'I could always . . . die!'

Then she knew that she wanted to live, to live her life fully and discover the world, and most of all, although she hardly dared to admit it to herself, she wanted to find love.

CHAPTER TWO

There was not a great distance between the Capital of Lützelstein and that of Dórsia, but the land was very mountainous and therefore the train in which they were travelling made, Zosina thought, a great to-do over it.

The whole journey, however, was so exciting that in retrospect even the long-drawn-out preparations seemed worthwhile.

She had not realised that she would require so many new clothes, until she found that they were to be part of her trousseau.

This made them less attractive than they had seemed when they were first ordered.

At the same time, because her sisters were so thrilled by the gowns, bonnets, sunshades, gloves, and of course the exquisite, sophisticated lingerie, Zosina found herself carried away as if on a tide.

Everything had to be done so quickly that she got very tired of fittings, and it was a relief to find that Helsa, although she was fifteen months younger, was a similar build to herself and could often "stand in" for her.

The only trouble was that every time she did so, Helsa was so envious that Zosina felt herself apologising humbly for being the chosen bride.

"It is not fair that the eldest should have everything," Helsa would say. "First, Papa likes you the best . . ."

"Which is not saying very much!" the irrepressible Katalin interposed.

"You get married first, and to a King!" Helsa finished.

"You might add that she is much the prettiest of us all," Theone said, "because that is the truth."

"If you only knew how much I wish this were not happening to me," Zosina said at length, when Helsa had been complaining for the hundredth time.

"The whole mistake has been," Katalin said, "that you are marrying a European. Now, if Papa had had the sense to choose a Moslem, such as an Arab or an Egyptian, he could have married off the four of us simultaneously!"

This made them laugh so much that the tension was broken, but Helsa's feelings only added to Zosina's own conviction that her marriage was not only going to be rather frightening but would separate her from her own family.

There was, however, nothing she could do, and she tried to tell herself that the gowns and the approval she was receiving from her father and mother were some compensation.

The Arch-Duchess, in fact, was so unusually affable that Theone said:

"If Mama was always in such a good mood as she is now, we would be able to suggest to her that we might occasionally have a dance or even just invite some friends to tea."

"I doubt if she would agree," Helsa said. "The sun is only shining at the moment because Zosina is to be a Queen."

It had certainly pleased her mother, Zosina thought, and she was rather surprised, because the Arch-Duchess had never appeared to be ambitious for her daughters.

Then it suddenly struck her that perhaps the real reason was that with her marriage she would be leaving home and there would be one less woman about the Palace.

Children seldom think of their parents as human beings.

So it was only during the last year that Zosina had seen her mother not as an authoritative, mechanical figure but as a woman with all the feelings and emotions of her sex.

It was then that she realised, with a perception she had never had before, that her

41

mother loved her father possessively and jealously.

On his side, as far as Zosina could ascertain, although he was scrupulously polite and courteous to his wife in public and consulted her in private, he showed no particular affection for her.

Now that she herself was to be married, Zosina found herself considering her father and mother as an example of two people whose marriage had been arranged for them and who, as far as the world was concerned, had made an excellent job of it.

Because she was looking for signs of deeper feelings than those which appeared on the surface, she realised, by the way her mother looked at her father, that beneath her almost icy exterior she was a frustrated and unhappy woman.

Looking back, Zosina recalled that at Court functions which they had been allowed to watch from the balcony in the Throne-Room or from the Gallery in the Ball-Room, her father had always singled out the most attractive woman with whom to dance or converse, once his official duties had been completed.

At the time she had merely thought how sensible he was to waltz with his arm round a lady who had a tiny waist and whose eyes sparkled as brightly as the jewels in her hair.

Now she wondered if the reason that there were so few entertainments in the Palace these days was the fact that her mother deliberately wished to isolate him from any contact with other women and keep him for herself.

She could understand how frustrating it was for her father no longer to be free to ride alone with a groom every morning, as he had done before his gout made him almost a cripple.

She felt certain too that he was not allowed to entertain any friends he might have away from the strict protocol of the Palace.

Vaguely, because she was so often daydreaming or engrossed in a book, she remembered little things being said about her father's attractions which should have given her an idea long ago that he had other interests in which his family did not share.

'Poor Mama!' she thought to herself. 'It must have been difficult for her to hide her jealousy, if that was what she was feeling.'

Then it struck her that she might find herself in the same situation.

It was all very well for Katalin to talk about her reforming the King, if he was a rake. But supposing she failed?

Supposing she did not reform him and spent her life loving a man who found her a bore and only wished to be with other women rather than herself?

When she thought such things, usually in the darkness of the night, she found herself clenching her hands together and wishing with a fervour that was somehow frightening that she did not have to go to Dórsia.

Most of all, she wished that she did not have to marry King György or any other man whom she had never seen.

'It is not fair that I should be forced into this position just because Germany wants to drag our two countries into her Empire!' she thought.

At the same time, she understood how desperately Lützelstein and Dórsia desired to keep their independence.

The might of the Prussian Army, and the behaviour of the Germans when they conquered the French, had made every Lützelsteiner violently patriotic and acutely aware that their own fate could be as quickly settled by a German invasion.

Zosina remembered how Lützelstein had been appalled when, nearly five years ago, King Ludwig of Bavaria had capitulated without even a struggle against the Prussian invitation to join the Federation.

Because Bismarck was so keen to have the King's approval, he had offered Bavaria an illusion of independence — she was to preserve her own railway and postal systems, to enjoy a limited diplomatic status in her dealings with foreign countries, and to maintain a degree of military, legal, and financial autonomy.

Zosina had so often heard the story of how, to be certain of the King's acceptance, it was even suggested that a Prussian and a Bavarian Monarch might rule either jointly or alternately over the Federation.

This had made the Lützelsteiners hope that things might not be as bad as they had anticipated.

Then disaster had struck.

There was talk of a Prussian becoming Emperor over a united Germany.

When the Prussian representative called to see King Ludwig, he was in bed, suffering from a sudden severe attack of toothache.

He did not feel well enough, the King said, to discuss such important matters, but somehow, in some mysterious manner, he was persuaded to write the all-important letter to his uncle, King Wilhelm I of Prussia, inviting him to assume the title of Emperor.

The fury that this had aroused in Lützelstein, Zosina thought now, must have been echoed in Dórsia.

All she could recall was that her father had stormed about the Palace in a rage that lasted for weeks, while Councillors came and went, all looking grave and disturbed.

This, she thought to herself now, was really the first step in uniting Lützelstein and Dórsia by a marriage between herself and the King.

She wondered if it had been in her father's mind ever since then, and she had the uneasy feeling that perhaps he and the Regent of Dórsia had been waiting until she and the King were old enough to be manipulated into carrying out the plan of alliance.

It was all so unromantic and so business-like in its efficiency that she thought cynically that no amount of pretty, frilly gowns could make her anything but the kind of "Card-board Queen" who was operated by the hands of power!

'I suppose the King feels the same,' she thought, but even that was no consolation.

She could almost see them both sitting on golden thrones with crowns on their heads, just like a child's toy, while her father with his Councillors, and the Regent with his, turned a key so that they twirled round and round to a tinkling tune, having no will and no impetus of their own.

"I suppose if I were stupid enough," Zosina said to herself, "I would take no interest in politics and would just be content to do as I was told and not want anything different."

She remembered how one of their Governesses had said to her:

"I cannot think, Princess Zosina, why you keep asking so many questions!"

"I wish to learn, *Fraulein*," Zosina had answered.

"Then confine yourself to subjects which are useful to women," the Governess had said.

"And what are they?" Zosina had enquired.

"Everything that is pretty and charming — flowers, pictures, music, and, of course, men," *Fraulein* had replied with a self-conscious little smile.

Zosina had not been surprised when soon after this the Governess, who was really quite attractive, was seen by her mother flirting with one of the Officers of the Guard.

She had been dismissed, and the Governesses who had followed her were all much older and usually extremely unattractive in their appearance.

Now, Zosina thought, it was not only the Governesses who were ugly but her mother's Ladies-in-Waiting and any other women who were to be seen frequently in the Palace.

Which raised the question that she had asked already as to whether this was intentional because of her father's interest in the fair sex.

"Surely it would be impossible for Mama to be jealous of me?" Zosina asked herself.

But she was not certain!

When she had gone down to the Study to show her father one of the new gowns that had been made for her State Visit, he had looked her over and said approvingly:

"Well, I may have been cursed with four daughters, but nobody could accuse them of being anything but extremely good-looking."

Zosina smiled at him.

"Thank you, Papa. I am glad I please you."

"You will please Dórsia, or I will want to know the reason why," the Arch-Duke replied. "You are a beauty, my girl, and I shall expect them to say so."

The Arch-Duchess had come into the Study at that moment, and when Zosina turned to look at her with a smile, she felt as if she were frozen by the expression on her mother's face.

"That will be enough, Zosina," she said sharply. "There is no need to tire your father, and do not forget that beauty is only skin-deep. It is character which will matter in your future position."

The way she spoke told Zosina too clearly that she thought that was a commodity of which she was lamentably short.

She had left the Study feeling that for the

first time she had really begun to understand what was wrong with the personal relationship between her father and mother and of course herself.

Every moment that she was not concerned with choosing, discussing, and fitting clothes, Zosina spent in thinking how much the company of her sisters meant to her.

It had been hopeless to try to explain to them that she felt the sands were running out and that once she had left the School-Room things would never be the same again.

Strangely enough, it was Katalin who realised that she had something on her mind. She came into her room after the others had gone to bed, to sit down and say:

"You are not happy, are you, Zosina?"

"You should not be up so late," Zosina said automatically.

"I want to talk to you."

"What about?"

"You."

"Why should you want to do that?"

"Because I can feel you are worried and I suppose apprehensive. I should feel the same."

Katalin made a little grimace as she went on:

"Helsa and Theone really want to be Queens and they do not care what they have to put up with so long as they can walk about with crowns on their heads. But you are different."

Zosina could not help laughing.

Katalin was such a precocious child, and yet she was far more sensitive than her other sisters and more understanding.

"I shall be all right, dearest," she said, putting out her hand to take Katalin's. "It is just that I shall hate leaving all of you and I am frightened I shall have nobody to laugh with."

"I should feel the same," Katalin replied. "But once the King falls in love with you, everything will be all right."

"Suppose he does not?" Zosina asked.

She felt for the moment that Katalin was the same age as she was and she could talk to her as an equal.

"You will have to try to love him," Katalin said, "or else the story will never have a happy ending, and I could not bear you to be like Mama and Papa."

Zosina looked at her in surprise.

"What do you mean by that?"

"They are not happy, anyone can see that," Katalin replied, "and Nanny told me once, before she left, that Papa loved somebody very much when he was young but he could not marry her because she was a commoner."

"Nanny had no right to tell you anything of the sort!"

"Nanny liked talking about Papa because she had looked after him when he was a baby. She thought the sun rose and set on him because he was so wonderful!"

That, Zosina knew, was true. Nanny had been already elderly when she had stayed on at the Palace to look after the girls when they were born.

Although it was reprehensible, she could not help being curious about her father and she asked:

"Did Nanny say who the lady was that Papa loved?"

"If she did I cannot remember," Katalin answered. "But she was very beautiful, and Papa loved her so much that the people were even frightened he might abdicate."

"How do you know all these things?" Zosina asked.

She could not help being intrigued.

"Nanny used to talk to the other servants who had been here almost as long as she had," Katalin replied, "and because they never liked Mama, they used to say all sorts of things when they forgot I was listening."

Zosina could believe that.

Nanny had been an inveterate gossip. She had not retired until she was nearly eighty, and had died two years later.

"Perhaps King György is like Papa," Katalin was saying, "in love with somebody he cannot marry. In which case, Zosina, you will have to charm him into forgetting her."

"I am sure he is too young to want to marry anybody."

Zosina spoke almost as if she was putting up a defence against such an idea.

"I expect that when they said he was wild, they meant there were lots of women in his life," Katalin said, "but they may be what Nanny used to call 'just a passing fancy.' "

"I cannot imagine what Mama would say if she could hear you talking like this, Katalin."

"The one thing you can be sure of is that she will not hear me," Katalin replied. "I am just warning you that you will have to be prepared for all sorts of strange things to happen when you reach Dórsia."

"It seems strange for you to be warning me," Zosina protested.

"Not really," Katalin replied. "You see, darling Zosina, you are so terribly impractical. You are always far away in your dreamworld and you expect real people to be like those you read about and like you are yourself."

"What do you mean by that?" Zosina asked.

"I have looked at the sort of books you read," Katalin said. "They are all about fantasy people who, like you, are kind, good, courageous, and searching for spiritual enlightenment. The people we meet are not like that."

Zosina looked at her young sister in astonishment and asked:

"Why do you say that about me?"

Katalin laughed.

"As a matter of fact, I did not think all that up about you, although it is true. It was what I heard *Frau* Weber say when she was talking to Papa's secretary."

"*Frau* Weber!" Zosina exclaimed.

Now she understood where Katalin got her ideas, because that particular Governess had been very different from all the rest.

A lady who had fallen on hard times, she had come to the Palace with an introduction from the Queen Mother.

She had been an extremely intelligent, brilliant woman, and her husband had been in the Diplomatic Service. When he died, she had been left with very little money and, as Zosina realised later, a broken heart.

The Queen Mother, who had always helped everybody who turned to her in trouble, had thought it would take her mind off what she had lost if she had young people round her.

As her granddaughters were in the process of inevitable change of Governesses, it had been easy for *Frau* Weber to fill the post.

Zosina realised at once how different her intellect and her ability to teach was from that of any Governess they had had before, and she felt herself respond to *Frau* Weber like a flower opening towards the sun.

However, her joy in being with somebody who could tell her so much that she wanted to know, and guide her in a way she had never experienced before, was short-lived.

An old friend of *Frau* Weber's husband came to Lützelstein on a diplomatic visit with the Prime Minister of Belgium and had renewed his acquaintance with the widow of his old friend.

When he left two weeks later, Zosina learnt in consternation that *Frau* Weber was to be married again.

"Then you will leave us!" she cried.

"I am afraid so," *Frau* Weber replied, "but I know I shall be happy with someone I have known for a great number of years."

The Arch-Duchess had been extremely annoyed that as a Governess, *Frau* Weber had made so short a stay in the Palace.

"It is most inconvenient and very bad for the girls to have so many changes," she said tartly to the Arch-Duke.

"We can hardly expect the poor woman to give up a chance of marriage for the doubtful privilege of staying here with us," he replied.

"I find people's selfishness and lack of consideration for others is very prevalent these days," his wife retorted.

It was Zosina who had cried when *Frau* Weber left, and she knew, as soon as she saw the woman who was to take her place, that she would never again find a Governess who understood how important knowledge was or how to impart it.

Thinking of her now, she said reminiscently:

"I wish I could talk to *Frau* Weber about my marriage."

"She is living in Belgium," Katalin said practically.

"Yes, I know it is impossible," Zosina replied, "but it would be pleasant to talk to somebody who understands."

"I understand," Katalin said. "You just have to believe it will all come right, and it will! Thinking what you want is magic. You do not have to rub an Aladdin's lamp or wave a special wand. You just have to focus your brain."

"Now who on earth told you that?" Zosina asked.

"I cannot remember, but I have always

known it," Katalin said. "I expect really it is the same as prayer. You want, and want, and want, until suddenly it is there!"

Zosina suddenly put her arms round her small sister and pulled her close.

"Oh, Katalin, I shall miss you so!" she said. "You always make even the most impossible things seem as if one can achieve them."

"One can! This is the whole point!" Katalin said. "Do you remember how Papa would not let us go to the Horse-Show, then suddenly changed his mind? Well, I did that!"

"What do you mean?" Zosina asked.

"I willed, and willed, and willed him, when I knew he was asleep at night or when I knew he was alone downstairs without anybody to disturb him, and quite suddenly he said:

" 'Why should you not go? It will do you good to see some decent horse-flesh!' So we went!"

Zosina laughed.

"Oh, Katalin, you make everything seem so easy! What shall I will for myself?"

"A husband who loves you!" Katalin replied without a pause.

Zosina laughed again.

It was in fact Katalin who made everything seem an adventure, even the moment when the Royal Train steamed out of the station, leaving three rather forlorn little faces waving good-bye from the platform.

"Good-bye, dearest Grandmama!" they had all said to the Queen Mother; then they hugged Zosina.

"You will have a lovely time," Theone prophesied.

"I wish I were you," Helsa said enviously.

But Katalin, with her arms round Zosina's neck, had whispered:

"Will, and it will all come right. Will all the time you are there, and I shall be willing too."

"I will do that," Zosina promised. "I do wish you were coming with me."

"I will send my thoughts to you every night," Katalin promised. "They will wing their way over the mountains and you will find them sitting beside you on your pillow."

"I shall be looking for them," Zosina said, "so do not forget."

"I will not," Katalin promised.

She waved from the window not only to her sisters but to the crowds of officials and their wives who were there to bid the Queen Mother farewell on what they all knew was a very important journey.

As the Royal Train was spectacular and, since the Arch-Duke had been confined to the Palace, very rarely used, crowds outside the station had come to watch it pass.

As she thought the people would be

pleased, Zosina stood at the window, waving, until her grandmother told her to sit beside her so that they could talk.

"I have hardly had a chance to see you, dearest child," she said, "and I must say you look very lovely in that pretty gown. I am glad you chose pink in which to arrive. It is always, I think, such a happy colour."

"You look lovely in your favourite blue, Grandmama," Zosina answered.

The Queen Mother looked pleased.

She was still beautiful, although the once-glorious red of her hair was now distinctly grey and her face, which had made a whole generation of artists want to paint her, was lined with age.

But her features and bone structure were still fine, and she had a grace which was ageless and a smile which Zosina thought was irresistible.

"Now, dearest," her grandmother was saying, "I expect your father has told you how important this visit is to our country and to Dórsia."

"Yes, he has told me that, Grandmama," Zosina answered.

There was something in her tone of voice that made her grandmother look at her sharply.

"I have a feeling, dear child, that you are

58

not as happy about the arrangements as you should be."

"I am trying to be happy about them, Grandmama, but I should like to have some say in my marriage, although I dare say it is very stupid of me even to think such a thing."

"It is not stupid," the Queen Mother said, "it is very natural, and I do understand that you are feeling anxious and perhaps a little afraid."

"I knew you would understand, Grandmama."

"I often think it is a very barbaric custom that two people, simply because it is politically expedient, should be married off without being allowed to say yes or no to such an arrangement."

Zosina looked at her grandmother. Then she said:

"Did that happen to you, Grandmama?"

The Queen Mother smiled.

"I was very fortunate, Zosina. Very, very fortunate! Have you never been told what happened where my marriage was concerned?"

"No, Grandmama."

Zosina saw the smile in the Queen Mother's eyes and on her lips as she said:

"Your grandfather, who was then the Crown Prince of Lützelstein, came to stay with my father because it had been suggested that he should marry my elder sister."

Zosina's eyes widened but she did not say anything.

"I was only sixteen at the time," the Queen Mother went on, "and very excited to hear that we were to have a Crown Prince as a very special guest."

She paused for a moment, as if she was recalling what had happened.

"It was naughty of me, but I was determined to see him before anybody else did," she went on after a moment. "So I rode from my father's Palace down the route to a point which I knew the Prince must pass when he entered the country."

"What happened, Grandmama?" Zosina enquired.

"I bypassed the welcoming parade of soldiers lining the streets by approaching the border from a different direction," the Queen Mother answered. "I had learnt that the Royal Party from Lützelstein, who had been travelling for several days, were to stop at a certain Inn just inside my father's Kingdom for refreshment, and of course to tidy up and make themselves look presentable before they entered our Capital in state."

Zosina was entranced by the story; she sat forward on the seat, her eyes on her grandmother's face.

"I often wonder how I had the temerity to do anything so outrageous," the Queen Mother said, "but I waited by some trees until I saw the Prince and his entourage come out of the Inn. They were laughing and talking, and their horses all stood waiting to be mounted."

"Then what did you do?" Zosina asked.

"I rode down to them at a gallop," the Queen Mother said. "I remember I was wearing a green velvet habit with a little tricorn hat, which I thought very becoming, with green feathers in it. I pulled my horse up right in front of the Prince. 'Welcome, Sire!' I said, and he stared at me in astonishment."

"It must have been a surprise!" Zosina cried.

"It was!" the Queen Mother replied, laughing. "Then I made my horse go down on his knees as I had trained him to do, and bow his head, while I sat in the saddle, holding my whip in a theatrical posture like a circus performer!"

Zosina was delighted.

"Oh, Grandmama! They must have thought it fantastic!"

"It was fantastic!" her grandmother said with a smile. "Your grandfather fell in love with me on the spot! He invited me to ride with him back to my father's Palace."

"And did you?"

"No. I was far too sensible to do that. I knew what a lot of trouble I would be in. I rode back alone, except of course for the groom who was waiting for me by the trees."

"And what happened after that?" Zosina wanted to know.

"When he reached the Palace, my sister was waiting for him and he said to my father:

" 'I understand Your Majesty has another daughter.'

" 'Yes,' my father replied, 'but she is too young to take part in our celebrations to commemorate Your Royal Highness's visit.'

" 'Will she not think it rather unfair to be left out of the celebrations?' your grandfather persisted."

"So you were allowed to take part," Zosina said.

"My father and mother were extremely annoyed," the Queen Mother replied, "but at the Crown Prince's insistence I came down to dinner. I remember how exciting it was, and even more exciting when, before the Prince left, he told my father that it was I he wished to marry."

"Oh, Grandmama, it is the most thrilling story I have ever heard!" Zosina exclaimed. "Why have I never been told it before?"

"I think," her grandmother replied, "your

mother thought it might put the wrong sort of ideas into your head."

"It is the kind of story Katalin would love," Zosina said. "I do wish I could tell her."

"Katalin knows already," the Queen Mother replied.

As Zosina looked at her in surprise she explained:

"Apparently she heard her Nurse gossiping about what had happened, and she asked me to tell her the true story."

"So you told her."

"Yes, I told her, but I made her promise to keep it a secret. I had to respect your mother's wishes in the matter."

"I am glad you have told me now," Zosina said, "and perhaps . . ."

She had no need to finish the sentence.

"I know what you are thinking — that perhaps King György will fall in love with you the moment he sees you, as happened to me," the Queen Mother said. "Oh, my dear, I hope so!"

"But suppose I do not fall in love with him?"

"Never think negatively," the Queen Mother advised. "Be positive that you will fall in love, and that is what I am quite certain will happen."

She did not wait for Zosina's reply but put

her hand against her granddaughter's cheek.

"You are very lovely, my child," she said, "and you will find that a pretty face is a tremendous help in life and in getting your own way."

Zosina laughed.

"Katalin told me I needed will-power to get what I wanted, and now you tell me it is being pretty."

"A combination of the two would be irresistible!" the Queen Mother said firmly. "So you have no need to worry, my dearest."

There was not much chance of further talk with her grandmother, because when they crossed the border from Lützelstein into Dórsia the train stopped at every station so that the Queen Mother could receive addresses of welcome from the local Mayors.

When they continued their journey there were crowds to wave and cheer when she and Zosina appeared at the windows of their carriage.

"The people are very pleased to see you, Grandmama," Zosina said.

"And to see you," her grandmother replied.

Zosina looked at her with a startled expression.

"Are you saying they know already that I am to marry their King?"

"I am quite certain the whole of Dórsia is

speculating as to why you have come and drawing their own conclusions," the Queen Mother replied. "In fact, if you had listened to that last address, which was an extremely dull one, the Mayor kept harping on the great possibilities that may come from this 'auspicious visit'!"

The way her grandmother spoke, which was a combination of irony and amusement, made Zosina laugh.

"Oh, Grandmama," she said, "you make everything so much fun! I love being with you! I only wish that you rather than I were marrying the King of Dórsia."

"There is a slight discrepancy in age to be considered," the Queen Mother remarked, "and as you well know, dearest, if it were not the King of Dórsia, it would be the King of somewhere else, or perhaps someone far less important."

"That is what Helsa is afraid she will get," Zosina said.

"We will do our best to find her a reigning Monarch," the Queen Mother said, "but they are rather few and far between, unless she has a partiality for one in the German Federation."

"None of us want that," Zosina objected.

"No indeed," the Queen Mother agreed. "Those small Courts are very stiff and starchy and one cannot breathe without offending protocol in one way or another. I am sure you girls would all hate it! I must say that the visits I paid there with your grandfather would have been absolutely intolerable if we had not been able to laugh, when we were alone, about everything that happened."

"Grandpapa must have been so glad he was able to marry you," Zosina said. "Do you ever wonder what would have happened if you had not been brave enough to go and meet him in such a manner?"

"Yes, I have often thought about it," the Queen Mother replied. "Someone else would have been Queen of Lützelstein, and perhaps, dearest, you would not all be so charming and so vital without my Hungarian blood in you."

"I have often thought that," Zosina agreed, "and I am sure it is why we all ride so well."

"Hungarians are born equestrians," the Queen Mother said. "I often teased your grandfather and said it was not me he fell in love with, but my horse, especially as he could do such splendid tricks."

"And what did Grandpapa reply?" Zosina asked.

The Queen Mother's eyes were very soft before she said:

"You are too young for me to tell you that, but one day you will learn what a man says

66

when he tells you what is in his heart."

There were more stations, more crowds, and the country with its mountains, its valleys, its distant snowy peaks, and its silver rivers had made Zosina know that the Ambassador had been right when he said it was one of the most beautiful places one could imagine.

There were lakes and Castles which made her think of the warring history of the early Dórsians, and then as the countryside became more populous she knew they were coming into the Capital.

She felt her heart begin to beat in a manner which told her she was frightened, and as the Ladies-in-Waiting began to fuss round the Queen Mother, giving her her gloves and her hand-bag and asking if she needed a mirror, Zosina thought almost for the first time of her own appearance.

She knew that her pink gown was exceedingly becoming, but somehow she suddenly felt gauche and insignificant beside the majesty and elegance of her grandmother.

"I must not make any mistakes," she said frantically to herself.

Then the train began to slow down and she saw that they were moving slowly into position at what appeared to be a crowded platform.

"Are you ready, my dearest?" the Queen Mother asked. "I will alight first, and you follow behind me. The King, and I expect too the Regent, will be waiting directly opposite the carriage door."

Zosina wanted to reply but her voice seemed to be strangled in her throat.

The train came to a standstill.

The Ladies-in-Waiting rose to their feet, and Zosina saw the Royal Party and several other gentlemen accompanying them pass in front of the window and knew they would be waiting at the door of the carriage.

Without hurrying, arranging her skirt to her satisfaction, the Queen Mother stood for a moment, determined, Zosina thought, to give a touch of drama to the moment when they would appear.

Then slowly, smiling her beguiling smile, she walked to the door of the carriage.

Zosina felt as if her feet had suddenly been rooted to the ground, and it was with considerable effort that she made them obey her.

The Queen Mother, assisted by willing hands, stepped down onto the platform; then almost without realising it, Zosina found herself behind her and a second later she heard a man's voice say:

"Welcome to Dórsia, Ma'am! It is a very

great pleasure and a privilege to have you here as my guest."

She thought the voice sounded young and rather boyish. Then the next moment the Queen Mother had moved on and Zosina curtseyed deeply as she took the hand that was waiting for her.

For a moment it was impossible to focus her eyes or to look up, and she heard the King say again:

"Welcome to Dórsia! It is a very great pleasure and a privilege to have you here as my guest."

Now she raised her eyes.

He was good-looking, and the miniature had been an excellent likeness, but there was something which the artist had omitted and which to Zosina was very noticeable.

It was the expression in the King's eyes, and she knew as she looked at him that he was staring at her with what she thought was resentment and, she was quite sure, dislike.

It was only a quick impression; then almost before it was possible to look at the King he had turned his face towards Count Csáky, who was directly behind her, and Zosina was forced to move on.

As she did so, she heard the Queen Mother say:

"I want you to meet my granddaughter,

the Princess Zosina."

Zosina curtseyed again, realising, as she did so, that she was now in front of the Regent, Prince Sandór.

It was difficult for a moment to think of anything but the way the King had looked at her and to know that her heart was thumping and she felt shocked because of what she had seen.

It was then that she felt her hand held in a firm grasp as a voice said:

"I am so very delighted, Your Royal Highness, that you are here, and I hope in all sincerity that we in Dórsia will be able to make your visit a very happy one."

There was no doubt that the voice was as sincere as the words.

As it flashed through Zosina's mind that she had no idea what the Regent looked like, she raised her eyes and saw that he was very different from what she had expected.

She had imagined, since he was uncle to the King and had been Regent for some years, that he would be old or at least middle-aged.

But there was no doubt that the man who held her hand as she rose from her curtsey was not much over thirty-three or -four.

He was good-looking, she thought, but in a different manner from the King, and there was an easy kind of self-confidence about him which seemed to Zosina to give her the assurance she needed at the moment.

It was as if he calmed and steadied her and the expression she had seen in the King's eyes did not seem so upsetting and frightening.

The Queen Mother was greeting the Prime Minister and various members of the welcoming party and for the moment Zosina made no effort to follow her.

Her hand still rested in the Regent's, and as if he knew what she was feeling he said:

"It is always rather bewildering to meet a whole collection of new people for the first time, but I can promise you, Your Royal Highness, they are all as delighted to see you as I am."

With an effort Zosina found her voice.

"You . . . are very . . . kind," she managed to say.

"That is what we all want to be," the Regent answered. "And now I want to introduce you to the Prime Minister, who is very eager to make your acquaintance."

There were more presentations, then the King was at the Queen Mother's side and they walked together with Zosina, following with the Regent, towards the door of the station.

As they reached it, a band began to play

Lützelstein's National Anthem, and it was followed by that of Dórsia.

By now they were standing four in a row, and out of the corner of her eyes Zosina could look at the King.

He was standing at attention and she thought that he was looking bored, and when the National Anthems were over and they stepped into the open carriage that was waiting for them, he yawned before he joined the Queen Mother on the back seat, while Zosina and the Regent sat opposite them.

As the horses started off amidst the cheers of the crowd, Zosina noticed that there were lines under the King's eyes and she told herself he must have been late to bed the night before.

'Katalin is right,' she thought. 'He is a rake, and I expect he thinks if he marries me I shall try to stop him from enjoying himself. That is why he dislikes me already, even before we have met.'

The idea was so depressing that for a moment she forgot to bow to the crowd.

Then she realised that the women, in particular, were staring at her and waving directly at her rather than at her grandmother.

With an effort she forced herself to respond.

As she did so, she realised that the King was looking at her again and there was no doubt that the expression in his eyes had not changed.

If anything, his dislike, if that was what it was, was intensified.

CHAPTER THREE

Zosina looked round the Dining-Room and wished her sisters were there.

It was certainly very different from the sombre, rather heavy room in which they dined at her father's Palace.

The light from the gold candelabra glittered on the profusion of gold plate, and the table was decorated with orchids, which also festooned the enormous marble fireplace and a number of the marble pillars.

It was a room, she thought, that might have stepped straight out of a fairy-story. She had also thought the same of the rest of the Palace, or rather of what she had been shown so far.

When she had first seen it standing above the town, white with the sunshine glittering on its windows and what appeared to be a gold dome over the centre of it, she had drawn in her breath.

It flashed through her mind that there might be some compensation in being the wife of a King who disliked her, if she could live in such attractive surroundings.

But even as she raised her eyes to the sun-capped mountains and looked at the green woods that covered the foothills behind the Palace and the flowering trees that lined the roads along which they were proceeding, she knew that the look in the King's eyes had caused a constriction in her heart that she could not control.

Without appearing to do so, she glanced at him, sitting opposite her, and realised that his hair was far darker than it had appeared in the miniature.

His skin was dark, and sun-burnt too, and his eyes, even apart from the expression in them, seemed almost black.

It made her remember that it was a joke amongst her sisters when they were angry to say to one another:

"Do not look at me with black eyes!"

That, she thought, described exactly the way the King looked at her.

Once they had entered the Palace and climbed up red-carpeted steps lined with soldiers in colourful uniforms, she forgot for a moment everything but the beauty of the building.

It was *Frau* Weber who had made Zosina study architecture and recognise the various periods.

Of course they had started with the Greeks, and Zosina had been so thrilled with the pictures of the Acropolis that she had felt that nothing could ever equal the symmetry and beauty of the Parthenon.

The Romans had delighted her too, and finally when they had reached the outstanding buildings erected by Robert Adam in the Eighteenth Century, she had longed, although she dared not say so, to pull down her father's Palace and erect something that she felt would be appropriate as a Royal Residence.

Here, almost like the answer to a prayer, was a Palace that embodied everything that she had ever admired.

Whoever had chosen the decorations inside had kept them uncluttered, free of fringes and tassels, and employed the vivid colours which Zosina knew always made her feel happy.

"I understand we shall be a very small party," the Queen Mother had said when they retired to their bedrooms to change for dinner. "Tomorrow there is a great Banquet being given in my honour and, although they do not say so, in yours, dearest."

Zosina did not reply and the Queen Mother went on:

"Tonight you will just meet the King's close relatives, although I expect the Prime

Minister and his wife will also be there."

She had made it sound quite intimate, but there were actually, Zosina counted, looking round the table, thirty people seated in what she had learnt was the private Dining-Room of the King.

The King had the Queen Mother on his right and Zosina was on his left.

On her left was the Regent and on his other side an extremely attractive, dark-haired woman with flashing eyes, who was talking to him intimately and making him laugh.

'I must not sit here dumb and saying nothing,' Zosina thought to herself, remembering how often her father had said:

"Nothing is more boring than taking into dinner a woman who is more concerned with her food than with oneself. It does not much matter what you say, but for Heaven's sake talk!"

Feeling a little shy because the King had not addressed a word to her since they had sat down, Zosina turned to him and said:

"I think, Sire, your Palace must be the most beautiful one in the whole of Europe!"

There was a little pause before the King looked at her, and she thought for one uncomfortable moment that he intended to ignore her remark.

Then he replied:

"You must be easy to please. I intend to make a great many alterations and certainly have it redecorated!"

"Oh no!" Zosina exclaimed involuntarily, thinking how lovely it was already.

Even as she spoke, she knew she had made a mistake, and once again the King was glaring at her with black eyes.

"If you think anybody is going to interfere with me once I am allowed to do what I wish," he said harshly, "you are very much mistaken."

He spoke so aggressively that Zosina gave a little cry before she said:

"Oh . . . please . . . I was not . . . meaning what you think I . . . meant. I only . . . thought the Palace was so . . . beautiful in every way, I cannot . . . imagine how it could be improved!"

Because she was embarrassed, her words seemed to tumble over one another as she attempted to explain herself.

The King merely remarked unpleasantly:

"You must be very easily pleased!"

He then turned deliberately to speak to the Queen Mother.

Zosina drew in her breath.

This was even worse than she had feared, and she told herself that she might have been tactless but she had not meant to upset him.

Then the Regent said to her:

"I heard you admiring the Palace. I am so glad that you find it attractive."

"I think it is . . . lovely."

"That is what I think too."

Because he seemed kind and understanding, she said in a low voice that only he could hear:

"I did not . . . mean to . . . upset His Majesty, and I was . . . trying to explain that I could not think how, as it looks so beautiful, it could be . . . improved."

The Regent smiled.

"We obviously think the same way," he said, in a tone which she knew was meant to be soothing.

Because she thought the subject must embarrass him if she continued with it, with an effort Zosina said:

"Count Csáky told me how beautiful Dórsia was, but I think it would be difficult even for the most accomplished poet to describe adequately what I have seen so far."

"You are fond of poetry?"

"Yes, very, but I know that some people find it . . . dull."

As she spoke, she was certain that the King would be one of them.

"I think poetry is rather like music," the Regent said quietly. "It can often express our feelings or our thoughts as ordinary words would be unable to do."

"It is strange you should think that," Zosina said with a sudden warmth in her voice. "Sometimes when I look at anything very beautiful I know that it would be impossible to describe it in prose and, as you say, only music or poetry could . . . say what it . . . makes me . . . feel."

She thought, as she spoke, that there was an expression of surprise in the Regent's eyes, but she was not sure.

Then, because she thought he would understand, she asked:

"May I ask you . . . something?"

"Of course," he replied.

"While I am here, could somebody tell me about Dórsia and its people?"

She paused a moment, then said quickly:

"I do not mean just its history, I mean the real human truths which one cannot . . . find in . . . books."

He did not speak, and, thinking he had not understood, she went on:

"It is like not being told how beautiful the Palace is before I came, or that the flowers are so brilliant and the people in the streets so colourful. I am frightened that if I am not looking out for what I should see, I might miss something important."

The Regent still did not reply, and after a second she said:

"I . . . I thought you would . . . understand . . . what I am trying to say."

"I do understand," he answered. "I understand very well. It is just that such a request has never been made to me before."

"Perhaps you . . . think it is the . . . wrong sort of . . . curiosity," Zosina murmured.

"It would be impossible for me to think that," the Regent replied, "because it is exactly what you should want to know."

She had a strange feeling that he was going to add: "But I had not expected you to do so," then deliberately prevented himself from saying it.

"What I will do while you are here," the Regent continued before she could answer, "is to try and give you what I believe is called a 'thumb-nail sketch' of the people you will meet and the places you will see."

He gave a little laugh before he added:

"I may not be as eloquent as some of our historical scholars or as indiscreet as the biographers of our important citizens, but I will certainly be shorter and, I hope, more informative."

"If you would . . . really do that," Zosina said, "I should be very . . . grateful. But I do not wish to be a . . . nuisance."

81

"You could never be that!" the Regent replied with a smile. "Now let me tell you a little about the people who are here at this table, and perhaps it would be politic to start with the Prime Minister."

He looked past Zosina down the table as he spoke, and she had a feeling that he deliberately missed out the King, who was sitting next to her.

He gave her, as he had suggested, a "thumb-nail sketch" of the Prime Minister, which not only made her laugh but at the same time made her aware of him as a man and also as a personality.

The Regent went on to one of the King's aunts, and he described her in a few words which made Zosina feel as if she were a character in a novel.

He spoke of two more people, then as he paused she said eagerly:

"Thank you, thank you, but do go on! You make everybody of whom you have spoken seem so real and also exciting to get to know. Please do not stop!"

"I am only too willing to go on," the Regent replied. "At the same time . . ."

As he spoke, he glanced towards the King and Zosina realised that she had committed a social error in talking to him for so long and not turning to the man on her other side, as she had been taught to do when at luncheon-and dinner-parties.

She was just about to say: "The King does not want to talk to me," when it struck her that the Regent perhaps wanted to talk to the very attractive lady on his left.

"I am . . . sorry," she said humbly. "I am being . . . selfish."

As she spoke, she turned her face towards the King, to find that he was sitting staring at the base of the candelabrum in front of him as if he had never seen it before.

It did not seem as if he wished to speak to her, but Zosina knew that she must make an effort, and after a moment she said in a nervous little voice:

"I was wondering . . . Your Majesty, what we will be . . . doing tomorrow. I know there is to be a . . . Banquet in the . . . evening."

"Then you know more than I do!" the King replied disagreeably. "You do not suppose I have had anything to do with arranging all this ballyhoo, do you?"

Zosina ignored his rudeness and said:

"I suppose State Visits and that . . . sort of thing must seem very . . . commonplace to you, Sire, but as I have never been on one before, I find it very exciting!"

"Exciting!" the King exclaimed. "I can tell you it is a deadly bore from start to finish. The only event slightly amusing might be the Masked Ball."

There was just a touch of interest in his voice, and Zosina said quickly:

"A Masked Ball sounds thrilling. Does it take place here in the Palace?"

"Good God, no!" the King replied. "It is for the people, not for us. We are supposed to sit on our gilded thrones, taking no part in it."

"How disappointing," Zosina said. "I have never been to a Masked Ball but I have heard of them, and it must be fun not to know whether you are dancing with a Count or a Candlestick-Maker, a King or a Chimney-Sweep!"

As she spoke, she hoped that what she said would make him laugh, but he turned to look at her with what she thought was a different expression from the one he had used before.

"Are you suggesting that I should go to the Ball?" he enquired.

"I may be wrong, Sire, but I have a . . . feeling you have been to . . . one already," Zosina replied.

He stared at her, not quite certain how to take what she had said. Then he said:

"You are trying to trap me. I am not going to answer that question."

"Of course I am not trying to trap you,"

Zosina answered. "If I were King I would certainly go to a Masked Ball, if I had the chance."

He did not reply, and after a moment she said:

"Now that I think of it, in history Kings have always gone about their countries in disguise. François I, for instance, used to go out every night, wandering round the town to mix with . . . his subjects."

She was going to say: "To mix with beautiful women," which was what she remembered reading in a somewhat racy French biography.

Then she thought that to say such a thing would not only be indiscreet but perhaps somewhat improper.

"Who was François I?" the King asked.

"He was the King of France, Sire, in 1515."

"I have never heard of him, but he obviously had the right ideas."

"Are you interested in history?"

"No, I am not!" the King replied. "I found it extremely dull and boring, but then I was never told anything interesting about the Kings, and certainly not the sort of thing you have just mentioned."

"One is not taught personal details about Royalty," Zosina replied. "One has to find it out in books."

"I have not time to read," the King said firmly.

They lapsed into silence and Zosina thought he was certainly very difficult. Perhaps the only person who could have coped with him would have been Katalin.

She would chatter on regardless of whether anybody answered her and always seemed able to find a new subject.

With almost a sigh of relief she saw the Queen Mother turn from the Prime Minister to speak to the King.

Almost as if she was unable to prevent herself, Zosina turned back to the Regent.

"Do tell me about the gentleman with the huge moustache," she pleaded.

She saw the Regent's eyes twinkling as he began the life-story of the gentleman who she learnt was one of the most redoubtable Generals in the Dórsian Army.

Afterwards, when the ladies withdrew to one of the exquisite Salons, Zosina found herself sitting next to one of the King's aunts, who she soon found was an irrepressible gossip.

The Princess chatted away about other members of the family, relating some of the most intimate details of their lives which Zosina was sure the Regent would not have told her.

"The woman with the dyed red hair is my cousin Lillie," she said. "She was very pretty ten years ago but now she is married to a terrible bore. What is more, he is deaf and everything has to be repeated three times. It also makes him shout until in his presence I feel I am permanently standing in a barrack square!"

Zosina laughed, then the Princess said in a low voice:

"And what, dear child, do you think of my nephew Györy?"

It was a question which Zosina was not expecting, and for a moment she found it difficult to find words in which to reply.

Then because she knew that the Princess was waiting she said:

"I did not . . . expect His Majesty to be so . . . dark-haired."

The Princess raised her eye-brows.

"Has no-one told you his mother was Albanian?"

"No," Zosina answered.

"Oh, dear, I see you have a lot to learn," the Princess said. "My brother, the late King, who was the eldest of eight children, had unfortunately four daughters by his first marriage."

"Like Papa!" Zosina remarked.

"Exactly!" the Princess replied. "And very

disagreeable it made him."

Zosina was about to say again: "Just like Papa!" but thought it would be indiscreet.

"When the Queen died," the Princess went on, "as you can imagine, it annoyed the Prime Minister and the Councillors when my brother announced that he intended to marry an Albanian Princess of whom none of us had ever heard."

"It must have been a surprise!" Zosina murmured.

"It certainly was, especially as we had always thought the Albanians to be a strange people, many of them being nothing but gypsies!"

There was so much disparagement in the Princess's voice that Zosina looked at her in surprise.

"However, my brother the King achieved what he had thought was an impossibility, when his second Queen produced a son and heir."

"He must have been very pleased," Zosina said.

As she spoke, she thought how thrilled her father would be if only he had a son to inherit the throne.

"You can understand," the Princess continued, "that Györy has naturally been very spoilt all his life. My brother doted on him until the day of his death, and his mother, in my opinion, spoilt him abominably."

The fact that the King was half-Albanian, Zosina thought, accounted for his dark hair and complexion, and it might also be the reason for his wildness.

As if the Princess followed her thoughts, she said:

"You have to be very understanding, dear, and gain Györgi's confidence. I believe, as does dear Sándor, that if he will settle down and assume his responsibilities he will make a good King."

At the mention of the Regent, Zosina said what had surprised her since she first arrived:

"I expected His Royal Highness to be much . . . older."

The Princess smiled.

"It does seem strange, as he is Györgi's uncle. But Sándor was the youngest of my father's large family of eight children, and my only other brother, and of course until Györgi arrived we always expected he would be the next King of Dórsia."

Zosina wanted to ask if he had been very disappointed at finding himself no longer the heir, but then she thought it would be a tactless question.

"All I can say," the Princess said, "is that you are not only very lovely, my dear, but exactly the sort of person we hoped you would be."

"Thank . . . you," Zosina replied, suddenly feeling shy.

Then before it was possible to say any more, the gentlemen came into the room.

The following day there were deputations of people calling on the Queen Mother from first thing in the morning until they had to leave the Palace for the Civic Luncheon that was being given for her by the Mayor and the Corporation of the City.

Once again they drove behind six white horses in the open carriage, and the crowds lining the roads seemed more enthusiastic than they had on the day of their arrival.

The Queen Mother had sent a message to Zosina by one of her Ladies-in-Waiting early in the morning to say that she was wearing pale mauve.

She suggested that Zosina should wear a white gown trimmed with lace and a bonnet wreathed with white roses.

"I look very bridal," Zosina remarked as she joined the Queen Mother in her bedroom before they proceeded downstairs.

"That is what you will soon be," her grand-mother replied.

Her words sent a shiver through Zosina, who had almost forgotten, in the excitement of all that had been happening, that the disagreeable and argumentative King was to be her future husband.

Thinking over his behaviour last night, after she had gone to bed, she had told herself that he was like a rather rude school-boy and it was difficult to think of him as a man.

She had always thought her husband would be somebody who would protect her and on whom she could rely, whose advice she would seek and who would direct her life in the way it should go.

She could not imagine finding any of these qualities in the King, and she thought that if she had to spend a lifetime trying to talk to him, that in itself was a terrifying prospect, especially if he was going to be as disagreeable as he had been last night.

However, because she wanted to do what was required of her and behave in an exemplary manner, she tried to excuse him on the grounds that they were strangers.

But she could not escape from the conviction that he disliked the idea of being married and more especially disliked the bride who had been chosen for him.

In which case, she thought, surely it would be better if he waited until he was older.

Then she remembered that the whole reason she was here was that Lützelstein and

Dórsia must be united if they were to oppose the growing power of Germany.

"I wonder if anyone has explained that to him?" she asked herself; then was certain that the Regent would have done so.

'Prince Sándor is clever,' she thought, 'clever and well read. At least he will be there for me to talk to.'

Then she wondered what happened when a Regent relinquished his post.

Did he retire into obscurity, or was another position found for him in the Government?

It was a question to which she did not know the answer, and she had a feeling it would be difficult to know who to ask.

The King looked sulky and bored all the way to the Guildhall where they were to be entertained.

He made no effort to speak to the Queen Mother or to anyone else, and Zosina, waving to the crowds who were obviously excited by her appearance, told herself that the only thing to do was to ignore him.

'He puts a damper on everything!' she thought. 'I cannot think, as this is his own country, why he does not enjoy seeing his people so pleased and excited.'

To her relief, when she reached the Guildhall she found that she was not sitting beside the King but had the Prime Minister on her left and the Chancellor of the Exchequer on her right.

She found that the thumb-nail sketches which the Regent had given her the night before were very helpful, although they seemed surprised that she should know how many children they had and, in the Prime Minister's case, that his wife was French.

They were soon talking animatedly and answering Zosina's questions about Dórsia in a manner which told her that they were extremely gratified by her interest.

"Thank you very, very much!" she exclaimed as she said good-bye to the Prime Minister. "It has been the most thrilling luncheon I have ever attended and I shall never forget it."

"You have made it a memorable occasion for me, Your Royal Highness," the Prime Minister replied, "and I can only assure you that you will find Dórsian hospitality is as boundless as our affection."

He spoke with an obvious pride in his voice, and as Zosina smiled at him he told himself that she was the most beautiful girl he had ever seen in his life.

When he said good-bye to the Regent, he added:

"I can only thank you as well as congratulate you, Sire, on your choice. You were far wiser than I was. I am therefore prepared, in the circumstances, never again to doubt your judgement, especially when it concerns women!"

The Regent's eyes twinkled.

"Shall I say I am thankful not to have made a fundamental mistake in this particular instance?"

"That, I can now say categorically, is an impossibility," the Prime Minister replied.

The Regent was still smiling as he hurried down the steps to take his place in the Royal Carriage.

When they got back to the Palace the Queen Mother announced that she was going to her private apartments.

"I hope, György, you will join me," she said to the King. "We have had no chance to talk intimately with each other since I arrived, so this is a welcome opportunity."

Zosina thought the King looked as if it was not a very welcome one to him, but it was obvious that there was nothing he could do but agree.

Having taken off her bonnet, Zosina went to the Queen Mother's Sitting-Room to find her grandmother waiting for her, and seated beside her, looking very sulky, was the King.

Zosina curtseyed and then the Queen Mother said:

"I am going to do something very uncon-
ventional, but I feel, as no-one will know
about it except ourselves, we can forget protocol for a moment. I want you two young people to get to know each other and so I am
going to leave you alone, without being
watched by curious eyes and listened to by in-
quisitive ears."

She gave the King and Zosina her famous
smile before, with a quickness of movement
which belied her years, she went from the
Sitting-Room, closing the door behind her.

Zosina, realising that the King had said
nothing, looked at him nervously.

He rose and walked across the room to
stand at the window looking out, and there
was an awkward silence until she said:

"Grandmama . . . always tries to make
things as . . . easy as possible."

"Easy!" the King replied, his voice rising on
the word. "I see nothing easy about your being here or this damned marriage!"

Zosina started when he swore, because
although she knew it was a swear-word she had
in fact never heard a man use it in her presence.

"Do you . . . hate the idea so . . . much?" she
asked falteringly after a moment.

"Hate it? Of course I hate it!" the King
snapped. "I have no wish to be married. All I
want is to be free — free of being ordered

about, free of being told what to do from morning until night."

"I can . . . understand your . . . feeling like that," Zosina said, "but you know why our marriage has been . . . arranged?"

"I know why they *say* it has been arranged," the King answered, "but the real truth is that Uncle Sándor wants someone to take his place, someone who will manipulate me as he has always done."

"I am sure that is not true," Zosina cried, "and if it were, they would not have chosen me!"

"That is *why* they have chosen you," the King said. "It is well known that your mother bosses your father and that Lützelstein has a petticoat Government."

"That is a lie!" Zosina protested. "Whoever told you that has deceived Your Majesty with a lot of rubbish!"

The King laughed and it was not a pleasant sound.

"It is a fact, whether you know it or not," he said, "and if you think you are going to rule my country, I promise that you will be disappointed!"

"I have no wish to rule anything or anybody!" Zosina said.

She saw that the King did not believe her, and after a moment she said more quickly:

"I did not wish to . . . get married either . . . I was merely . . . told that I had to do so."

"Do you expect me to believe that?" the King asked. "Every woman wants a crown on her head."

"Then I am the exception," Zosina said. "I want to . . . love the man I marry."

The King laughed jeeringly.

"Love is a cheap commodity . . ." he said. "There is plenty of it about, but one cannot marry it. Oh no! That is arranged by one's Councillors, or in my case by my uncle."

He spoke in a manner which told Zosina that he hated the Regent.

She had been standing while they were talking, but now she sat down in a chair as if her legs would not support her.

"What . . . can we . . . do?" she asked helplessly.

"Do?" the King questioned. "What we are told to do, of course! Uncle Sándor has it all neatly tied up, while the Prime Minister and all those idiotic creatures who kow-tow to him behave as if I were a performing animal in a circus: 'Jump through a hoop, Your Majesty!' 'Turn a somersault, Your Majesty!' 'Fly on the trapeze, Your Majesty!' You do not suppose I have any chance of refusing them?"

Zosina clasped her fingers together.

"I know it seems . . . unfair . . . and perhaps

cruel," she said in a small voice, "but the menace of the . . . German Empire is real . . . very real!"

"That is what they tell you," the King answered. "Personally, I do not care a damn if the Germans do incorporate us in their Empire. We would very likely be better off than we are now."

"No! No!" Zosina cried. "How can you say such a thing? We have to keep our independence. How could we be ruled by a Prussian Emperor?"

"He would leave me on my throne."

"For as long as you did what you were told," Zosina said. "If you think you are badly off now, it is nothing to the position you would find yourself in under the Germans."

"Now you are talking like Uncle Sándor," he said with a sneer. "I think it is all a lot of 'bogey-bogey' thought up by politicians who have nothing better to do!"

"Oh, it is real . . . it is true," Zosina insisted. "I read the newspapers and I have also heard what my father says about the menace of the German might. We cannot let Lützelstein and Dórsia come under Prussian rule!"

"All I want," the King replied, "is to enjoy myself and to have a good time. If I tried to interfere in politics they would soon stop me, so what is the point of my wasting my time trying to understand them?"

Zosina gave a little sigh.

The King, she thought, was more than ever like a truculent school-boy, and she had the feeling he was so angry that whatever she said, he would never understand the seriousness of the situation or believe that she was not trying to manipulate him in some manner.

She rose to walk across the room and stand not beside him but at the next window, looking out as he was.

The sunshine made the snow on the peaks of the mountains a dazzling white against the blue of the sky, and she thought she could see the cascades of water running down the sides of the hills.

In the distance, the river which passed through the city flowed like a silver streak towards the horizon.

"Dórsia is so lovely," she said, "and it is yours. It belongs to you!"

The King laughed loudly.

"That is what you think, but the person who rules it is Uncle Sándor, and everyone from the Prime Minister to the lowest crossing-sweeper knows it."

His voice had a jeering note in it as he went on:

"Have you not been told by now that I am an unfortunate 'after-thought'? The son of an

Albanian gypsy who ought never to have got into Dórsia in the first place?"

"You are the King," Zosina replied, "and surely it is up to you to gain the love and respect of your people. When you have done that — and kept your country free — you may justifiably feel very proud of yourself."

The King laughed again, and this time there was a note of genuine amusement in his voice.

"Now you are really starting in the way you mean to go on," he said. " 'You must be a good King!' 'Be kind to your people!' 'They must learn to love you!' 'You must do the right thing!' "

He threw up his hands in a gesture that was somehow derisive.

"Uncle Sándor has done it again!" he said jeeringly. "He has picked the right 'petticoat' to rule Dórsia . . . and who could have learnt how to do it better than a Princess who comes from Lützelstein?"

Zosina felt her temper rising.

"I think you are being needlessly insulting!" she said. "If I could do what I wish to do, I would go back to Lützelstein, stay with my father, and tell him I will not marry you when everything I say or do is suspect!"

"So you have got a temper!" the King said. "Well, that is better than all that mealy-mouthed preaching anyway."

Zosina suddenly realised that she was being almost as rude and angry as he was.

"I am . . . sorry," she said with genuine humility. "I do not wish to preach . . . and I promise you I do not wish to coerce you into doing anything you do not want to do."

"But you will, all the same," the King said, "and you will do it for my own good."

Again his voice was jeering before he went on:

"That is what Uncle Sándor always says: 'I am only telling you this for your own good!' If you want the truth, I am sick to death of my uncle and anyone else for that matter! I want to be left alone! I want to enjoy myself, have fun with my own friends, make love to the women I choose — and let me tell you once and for all — you are not my type!"

Zosina was tempted to snap back that he was not her type either, but she knew it would sound very childish.

Instead, she just stood staring blindly out the window, feeling that this could not be happening. In fact, the whole conversation was like something in a nightmare.

"I will tell you one more thing," the King said loudly. "If we have to marry, and I cannot see how I can get out of it, the moment I am properly a King and can send Uncle

Sándor packing, I shall go my way, and you can go yours!"

As he spoke he walked across the Sitting-Room and left, slamming the door behind him.

Zosina put her hands up to her face, feeling that this could not be true, and if it was, then perhaps it was all her fault.

"How did I manage to upset him? Why did I make him angry?" she asked herself.

She could feel her hands trembling against her cheeks and knew that her whole body was trembling too.

She found it difficult to think or really to believe that the King had been so rude.

Never in her life had a man, with the exception of her father, spoken to her in a horrible jeering voice which, like a squeaking saw, seemed to set her nerves on edge.

'How can I marry anybody like that?' she thought, and felt a sudden panic sweep over her.

It was then that the door opened and a servant announced:

"His Royal Highness the Prince Regent, Your Majesty!"

Zosina put out her hand to hold on to the window-ledge.

She could not turn round. She could not face the Regent, and yet she knew that, having entered the room, he must be staring at her back, in surprise.

Then she heard the door shut and after a moment his voice, quiet and calm, as he said:

"What has happened? Why are you alone? I saw the King coming away from here."

Zosina tried to find her voice and failed. Then she was aware that he had crossed the room.

"You are upset," he said quietly. "I am very sorry if the King has done anything to disturb you."

He sounded so kind that Zosina felt the tears come into her eyes.

Then as if she could not prevent the words, she heard herself say:

"He hates me! He is very . . . angry because you . . . brought me . . . h-here!"

She felt that what she had said surprised the Regent.

"I cannot believe the King said that he hates you," he replied. "What did he actually say?"

"I . . . I c-cannot repeat it," Zosina said quickly, "but he resents having . . . to . . . to marry, and he thinks that you chose me because . . . I would . . . boss him as he said . . . M-Mama does Papa."

The words came out without her really meaning to say them, and as she spoke a tear from each eye ran down her cheeks.

She hoped the Regent would not notice, and she went on staring blindly ahead at the mountains, which now she could not see.

The Regent came nearer still and now he was standing at her side, looking at her, and she felt for some strange reason that she could not explain that she must not move; must not even breathe in case he learnt too much.

"I am sorry," he said at length in his deep voice. "Desperately sorry that this should have happened, and to you of all people."

"Please . . . can I go . . . home? Perhaps you could . . . find somebody else?"

She was afraid as she spoke the last words, and yet she said them.

"You know that is impossible," the Regent answered. "Although it seems a hard thing to say, this marriage, because it concerns our two countries, is more important than an individual's likes or dislikes."

"The . . . King does not seem to be . . . aware of that," Zosina murmured.

"He must understand it by now," the Regent said, and there was a sharp note in his voice. "The whole situation has been explained to him over and over again."

"He wants to be . . . free."

"Which is something he certainly would not be under the Emperor Wilhelm."

"That is . . . what I told him . . . but he would not listen."

The Regent sighed.

"I think perhaps he is just being difficult."

"Surely you could have . . . allowed him to . . . find his own wife?" Zosina questioned. "Perhaps he would have . . . fallen in love with . . . one of my sisters, if he had come to . . . Lützelstein."

The Regent did not reply and after a moment she turned to look at him and their eyes met.

The tears were still on her cheeks, but now she could see more clearly and there was an expression in his eyes that she did not understand.

"I am . . . sorry," she said after a moment, "but I am a . . . failure. You can see . . . I am a . . . failure."

"You are nothing of the sort," the Regent replied. "It is all my fault, but even now that I have met you, I am not certain I could have done anything different."

He saw that Zosina did not understand and after a moment he said:

"I did not expect you to be as you are."

"Why am I . . . wrong?"

There was something almost pathetic in the question, and the Regent said hastily:

"But you are not wrong! You are right, absolutely right in every way. It is just that this situation is something in which you should never have been involved. I cannot understand why I did not realise it — but then, I had never seen you!"

"What did you not . . . realise?" Zosina asked.

"That you would be sensitive, vulnerable, and far too intelligent."

Zosina's eyes widened.

"H-how do you . . . know I am . . . that?"

"You forget, we have talked together," the Regent replied.

"Then if you . . . think I am all . . . those things . . . why am I . . . wrong?"

For a moment she thought he would not answer. Then he said almost abruptly:

"I thought you would be like your mother!"

Zosina drew in her breath.

"The King said that . . . everybody knows that . . . Mama rules Lützelstein and it is a . . . petticoat Government."

The Regent's lips tightened.

"He had no right to say such a thing."

"But it is . . . what you . . . think?"

"I have not said so."

"Is it true? I had no idea. Papa always seems so overpowering to me and my sisters that I imagined he overwhelmed . . . everybody else in Lützelstein."

Even as she spoke, it struck Zosina that perhaps the reason why her father was so disagreeable and overbearing to her and her sisters was that outside the Palace his wife forced him into making the decisions she wanted.

But even now she could hardly believe that the King had not talked nonsense.

Then she asked herself helplessly how, sitting in the School-Room, could she possibly have known what went on in the Council Chambers and what decisions her father made on the many problems that were brought to the Palace day after day by members of the Government.

For the first time it struck her that her mother always seemed to have an opinion on everything.

Because she and her sisters were frightened of her and of their father, they seldom if ever voiced an opinion of their own in the presence of their parents.

She thought now that that was what the Regent wanted to happen in Dórsia and the King was right.

He had chosen her because he thought she would be strong and determined and would force the King into doing things he did not want to do and against which he was obviously rebellious.

"I cannot do . . . anything like . . . that," she said in a whisper.

She felt, as she spoke, that the Regent had been following her thoughts and understood exactly what she was saying.

"I know that now," he said. "But it is too late."

"Why?"

"Because the Prime Minister and the Cabinet have agreed that you should marry the King. The Councillors who have met you already are simply delighted with you. They see you as somebody very beautiful, very compassionate, someone whom the country will love, which is very important."

"What . . . about the . . . King?"

It was difficult to say the words, and yet they were said.

"I will make the King behave himself," the Regent replied, and his voice was hard.

"No, no . . . please!" Zosina cried. "Do not antagonise him! He hates me . . . he resents me. If he learns I have complained to you, it will only make things . . . worse."

"Then what can I do?"

She thought that he felt as helpless as she did.

"It would be . . . better to do . . . nothing," she said. "I will try . . . really try . . . to make him . . . trust me . . . and then perhaps things will be . . . different."

As she spoke, she thought that the King was almost like a wild animal she had to tame. The first thing she must do was to prevent him from shying away at her approach, suspecting that she was trying to capture and imprison him.

Then she remembered that the King was not an animal but a man and she was very ignorant about men.

Every instinct in her body shrank from having anything to do with one who swore and jeered at her. The things the King had said made her wince even to remember them.

Her face must have been very expressive, for the Regent said:

"Forgive me, please forgive me for creating this tangle. I see now only too clearly what I have done, but I do not know how to undo it."

There was a note of humility in his voice and at the same time a sympathy and compassion that had not been there before.

"There is . . . nothing you can do," Zosina said. "I am aware that it is . . . up to me . . . but please help me and . . . if you can . . . give me courage . . . because I am . . . afraid."

Without really realising what she was doing, as she spoke she put out her hand towards him, and he took it in both of his.

"I do not believe that any woman could be more brave or more wonderful!" he said quietly.

Chapter Four

For what seemed to Zosina a long time she looked into the Regent's eyes. Then in a voice which seemed to her to come from a long way away she whispered:

"Thank . . . you."

As she spoke, the door opened and the Queen Mother came back into the Sitting-Room.

She looked in surprise at the Regent as he released Zosina's hand and asked:

"Where is György? I thought he was here."

"He had an audience which he had forgotten, Ma'am," the Regent replied.

"How like György!" the Queen Mother remarked. "But I think that since I last saw him he is much improved. I congratulate you, Sándor. I know how difficult it has been."

As she finished speaking she glanced at Zosina in a way that made her sure that her grandmother had forgotten she was in the room.

The Queen Mother then paused and said in a different tone:

"I am sure, dear child, it would be a good idea if you rested before this evening. I want you to look your very best at the State Banquet."

"I will go and lie down, Grandmama."

Zosina curtseyed and kissed her grand-mother's cheek. Then she dropped a curtsey to the Regent, feeling, as she did so, that it was impossible to look at him.

In her bedroom she found a programme of future events left on a *secretaire* and knew that it had been put there by one of the Aides-de-Camp who had been looking after them since they arrived.

It contained, besides the events at which they were to be present, a list of the important people they would meet and their positions.

Zosina picked it up absent-mindedly because her thoughts were elsewhere.

When she glanced down to see at what time she had to be ready tonight for the State Banquet, she read:

11:30 A.M. *H.M. Queen Szófia and H.R.H. Princess Zosina to inspect the Convent of the Sacred Heart.*

2:30 P.M. *H.M. Queen Szófia to open the new Botanical Gardens.*

7:00 P.M.   *H.M. The King, H.M.*
Queen Szófia, H.R.H.
Princess Zosina, H.R.H. The
Prince Regent, will dine with
the Members of the Order of
St. Miklos.

These, she knew, were all noblemen of
Dórsia. Then an entry for the next and last
day made her draw in her breath:

11:00 A.M.   *Reception by the Prime*
Minister in the House of
Parliament, where all the
Members will be assembled.
On this occasion the King's
impending marriage will be
announced.

Zosina put down the programme and
walked across her bedroom to sit on the stool
in front of the dressing-table.

For a moment she saw her reflection not
with her hair elegantly and fashionably arranged but with a glittering crown on her
head.

This was why she had come to Dórsia; this
would be her future.

She gave a little cry and put her hands up to
her eyes.

How could she endure it — not being Queen of such a charming and friendly people, but being the King's wife?

She felt as if it were a trap from which there was no escape; her thoughts were going round and round like a squirrel in a cage which knew there was no way out, and she felt as if she would go on turning and turning until she died.

Then, almost as if he was again standing beside her, she could hear the Regent say:

"I do not believe that any woman could be more brave or more wonderful!"

"That is what I have to be," she told herself, and quickly looked away from the mirror in case she should see the crown again.

The State Banquet was certainly impressive.

In the Banqueting-Hall of the Palace over three hundred guests sat down to a very elaborate dinner with eight courses and appropriate wines for each one.

It would be impossible, Zosina thought, for anyone to look more magnificent or more regal than her grandmother.

Wearing some of the Lützelstein Crown Jewels which she had brought with her especially for the occasion, her gown glittering with diamanté, and with five ropes of huge diamonds round her neck, she looked like every woman's ideal of a Queen.

Zosina felt that in contrast she must pale into insignificance.

Her gown, instead of being white, which she knew was being kept for her wedding, was the second most elaborate one in her trousseau.

Of very pale blue, the colour of the morning sky, it had a tulle train which frothed out behind her like the waves of the sea, and tulle encircled her shoulders, accentuating the whiteness of her skin and making her eyes seem unnaturally large in her small face.

As a concession to her impending marriage, the Grand-Duchess had lent her one of the small tiaras which had always been considered too unimportant for her to wear herself.

It was in fact a wreath of flowers fashioned in diamonds and turquoises, and as it glittered and shimmered under the huge crystal chandeliers it made Zosina, although she was not aware of it, look like the Goddess of Spring.

There was a necklace of diamonds and turquoises to match, and bracelets for her wrists.

When she was dressed she wished that her sisters could see her, especially Katalin.

Katalin had had a great many amusing

things to say about her gowns before she left Lützelstein.

"You will look exactly like the Prima Donna in an Opera!" she had exclaimed. "Except, of course, you have not a large enough bosom to be a singer! But doubtless the King will be bowled over by your beauty the moment he sees you."

'Well, that at least is something that will not happen!' Zosina thought now.

She hoped, however, that the Regent would think she was appropriately dressed for the part she had to play, and perhaps if she tried very hard she could at least charm the King into being polite to her.

In a way, she could understand how he resented being under the authority of his uncle. After all, he was the King, and to have someone else, however pleasant, ruling for him must be frustrating.

She thought of how her mother had always insisted that they should take no part in any of the celebrations that took place in Lützelstein, except those which involved their going to a special Church Service or standing on a balcony to watch a procession pass beneath them.

Now that the idea that her mother was bossy had been put into her head, Zosina began to remember dozens of occasions when her mother had overruled her father's wishes or forbidden them some treat which he would have given them only too willingly.

"A petticoat Government!" she whispered to herself, and wondered how she could make the King understand that she had no wish to boss anyone, least of all him.

'I want to get to know the people,' she thought, 'and, as the Regent said, for them to love me.'

It was in fact terrifying that those who had brought her to Dórsia had done so because they thought she would keep the King in order and influence him from behind the throne.

It made Zosina feel almost panic-stricken to think that the plan was that anything that happened in the country would be done at her instigation or because she could influence the King into the right way of thinking.

"I am quite certain of one thing," she told herself. "Whatever I suggest, he will do the opposite, just out of spite."

Then she told herself that that was not how Katalin would tackle the problem.

'I have to will him into listening to me,' she thought.

She wondered if Katalin's idea of "willing" for what one wanted could ever really be possible in ordinary, every-day life.

Then she remembered how positive Katalin had been that it would work.

"First I must will him into believing that I am not dangerous or obstructive," Zosina told herself, "but sympathetic and understanding."

Then she knew that as far as she was concerned it would be a question of praying rather than willing the King to do anything.

"God will help me," she whispered.

At the same time, she felt she was weak because she knew she would not rely on herself but only on the Power to whom even miracles were possible.

As she walked along the corridor with her grandmother to go downstairs to the State Banquet, the Queen Mother said with her usual kindness:

"You look lovely, my dear! Everybody in Dórsia is captivated by your beauty and your charm, and I am very proud of you."

"Thank you, Grandmama."

"What was Sándor saying to you when I came into the room?"

There was an undoubted note of curiosity in the Queen Mother's voice, but Zosina thought it would be impossible to tell her what the Regent had been saying or to relate their conversation when he had found her in tears.

After an infinitesimal pause she replied:

"His Royal Highness was talking about the King, Grandmama."

The Queen Mother smiled.

"I thought it must be something of the sort, and I am sure you will find that you and György have a great many subjects in common. After all, you are practically the same age. He needs a young companion when he has so many State duties to perform."

Zosina thought that while this was true, she was not the companion he needed.

At the State Banquet she was dismayed to find that because the King was the host and she and her grandmother were the Guests of Honour, they were once again seated on his right and left.

As the dinner began, Zosina was at first so fascinated with looking at the beauty of the scene that she could think of nothing else.

Again, a profusion of exotic flowers decorated all the tables, which were also laden with magnificent ornaments of gold and silver.

Enormous crystal chandeliers which held hundreds of lighted candles sparkled overhead.

There were too, Zosina noticed, as a concession to progress, a number of gas-globes in the room, which she was sure was the regular way of lighting the enormous Banqueting-Hall except on very special occasions.

Tonight the candlelight was very becoming and she thought that the ladies of Dórsia had a beauty which certainly exceeded those of her own country.

The men too were extremely handsome, tall and broad-shouldered, with clean-cut features, like the Regent.

He was seated on her left, and as if he read her thoughts, he asked as she stared round her:

"Do we pass muster?"

She turned to smile at him and he saw that her eyes were shining with excitement.

"It is all so beautiful!" she exclaimed. "And I was thinking that the people of Dórsia are beautiful too."

"You are very flattering," he replied, "and I am sure the Queen Mother would claim it is due to the preponderance of Hungarian blood in our veins!"

"Of course that could account for it," Zosina agreed.

"Also due to our Hungarian ancestors," the Regent went on, "you will find a great many Dórsians are red-headed and fair-skinned."

Zosina longed to add: "It is a pity that the King should have inherited the Albanian appearance of his mother rather than that of his Dórsian father."

Instead she remarked:

"I have never been to a State Banquet before. I feel it is rather like taking part in the most glamorous and exciting production in a Theatre."

She remembered that Katalin had said that she looked like a Prima Donna in an Opera, and it crossed her mind that if her sister could see the Regent she would certainly think he qualified as the leading man.

Tonight, like the King, he was wearing a white tunic, but as his was a military one, it had heavy gold epaulettes and his collar was also embroidered with gold.

While the King's decorations were those traditionally worn by a Monarch, many of the Regent's were battle honours which Zosina recognised from those she had been shown when she was inspecting the Armoury in the Palace.

There was also something in his bearing and his air of authority that told her he would be a good commander in the battlefield and certainly a leader of men.

He pointed out to her one or two celebrities amongst the diners; then, because she knew she must do what was expected of her, she turned politely to the King, who sat on her other side.

For a moment it seemed impossible to think of anything to say, and she thought that if she annoyed him they might start fighting again.

Because it was the first uncontroversial thing that came into her mind, she asked:

"Do you ever give Balls at the Palace? This would be a lovely room in which to dance."

"We do have them, but they are very formal and boring," the King replied in a rather surly voice.

There was a pause, then he added:

"But I will soon change all that."

"It would certainly be fun to have a Ball," Zosina said, trying to be agreeable.

"Not if the guests are all as decrepit as these creatures!" he said, looking fiercely at the people dining with them.

Zosina was about to say instinctively: "Do be careful in case they should hear you!" then realised it would be a rebuke which the King would undoubtedly resent.

Instead she said:

"I am sure, Sire, you have a great many young friends who would enjoy dancing, as I do."

"I have," the King answered. "But you do not suppose I am allowed to invite them here? Oh no! My friends are not good enough for Uncle Sándor!"

Zosina gave a little sigh.

They were back on the subject of his dislike of authority and especially that of his uncle.

There was a pause when she could think of nothing to say. Then the King remarked:

"If you want to dance and meet my friends, you can come with me tonight."

"Come . . . with you?" Zosina asked. "Where?"

"To the Masked Ball."

Zosina stared at him in astonishment.

"The . . . Masked Ball? It is taking place tonight?"

The King nodded; then, with a note that was almost one of enthusiasm, he said:

"It will be very different from this! I am meeting my friends there when all this ceremony and pomposity is over."

Zosina looked at him wide-eyed, and he said:

"Are you sporting enough to come with me, or are you too afraid to play truant?"

There was a jeering note in his voice, as if he knew her answer without her giving it.

"What are you . . . suggesting I . . . do?" Zosina asked almost in a whisper.

"You will have to slip out when everybody has gone to bed," the King answered. "That is what I always do."

"And you will . . . take me to a . . . Masked Ball?"

"I bet you are not brave enough to come!"

It was a challenge, Zosina thought, rather of the type of "dare" in which her sisters, especially Katalin, indulged, and which had often made her afraid.

"I bet you are not brave enough to walk along the parapet!" "I bet you are not brave enough to climb over the roofs!"

They were the sort of "dares" that had always made her frightened, and yet she had often forced herself to undertake them just so that the others would not think her a spoil-sport.

But this was an even greater "dare," and she knew how angry the Queen Mother would be if it was discovered that she had left the Palace unchaperoned.

And yet, in a way, this was the chance she had been looking for, to make the King feel that she was not against him but sympathised with and understood his difficulties.

There was a cynical twist to his lips and she was quite sure that he felt she was far too cowardly and conventional to accept his invitation.

It was then that she suspected he had offered it merely as an act of defiance because he knew it was so outrageous.

Zosina made up her mind.

"I will . . . come!" she said. "If you can

make quite . . . certain it is not . . . discovered.
I know Grandmama would be very . . . angry,
and so, I am sure, would the Prince Regent."

The King laughed.

"You bet he would! In fact, he would stop
me if he had the slightest suspicion of what I
was up to."

"You have done this sort of thing before?"
Zosina enquired.

"Dozens of times!" the King boasted. "And
nobody has ever yet caught me!"

Zosina felt a little tremor of fear that this
might be the first time, but aloud she said:

"I think it is very courageous of you! But
supposing you are recognised?"

"No chance of that," the King said. "You
have forgotten, we will be masked."

"How can I get one?" Zosina asked.

"I will see to that," the King replied, "if you
are sure you have the guts to come with me."

It was a rather vulgar way of putting it,
Zosina thought, but it summed up exactly what
she needed in order to do something which she
was well aware could land her in a great deal of
trouble and which would outrage her father and
mother if they ever heard about it.

"I will . . . come!" she said, with a little
quiver in her voice, "but please let us be very
. . . careful and make sure . . . nobody sees
us."

"If you do exactly as I tell you," the King said, "it will be quite safe, but do not go squealing afterwards, if it turns out not what you expect and you do not like being outside your gilded cage."

Again he was sneering. At the same time, Zosina thought, he was really rather pleased that she had accepted his invitation.

Then she knew the reason when he said:

"We are really putting one over Uncle Sándor! He thinks he has got your whole visit well buttoned up, down to the last detail! Well, I am ready to show you he is wrong!"

"You will . . . not tell him . . . afterwards?" Zosina asked nervously.

"And have one of his interminable lectures?" the King questioned. "I am not such a fool as to do that, but I shall feel jolly cock-a-hoop that I can outwit him."

Zosina realised that because he was obsessed with the subject of his uncle's authority, he found it impossible to talk of anything else.

Aloud she said:

"Tell me more details . . . later. I think I must now talk to the Prince Regent."

"Leave everything to me," the King said.

Zosina turned her head to find the Regent waiting to speak to her.

"I want tomorrow to show you what I think are rather beautiful pictures painted by one of the Nuns in a Convent," he said, "which is situated high in the mountains."

"I would love to see them," Zosina replied.

"A number of extremely intelligent and talented women live in this particular Convent," the Regent went on, "and one of them is a poetess, I have had her poems bound and I am going to have a copy of them put in your bedroom. Perhaps before you go to sleep tonight you will glance through them. I am convinced you will find them very moving."

"How kind of you!" Zosina exclaimed. "You know I love poetry."

"As we have said before, poets can often say for us things that are impossible to express in any other way," the Regent remarked. "Perhaps one day — somebody will write a poem to you."

Zosina had the strange feeling that he had been about to say: "*I* will write a poem to you."

Then she told herself that she had been mistaken and there had not been a perceptible pause before the word "somebody."

She was looking again at the guests sitting at the flower-decorated tables when the Regent quoted:

*"And bright
The lamps shone o'er fair women and brave
    men;
A thousand hearts beat happily."*

"Lord Byron!" Zosina laughed and continued:

*"And when
Music arose with its voluptuous swell,
Soft eyes look'd love to eyes which spake
    again,
And . . ."*

She stopped as she suddenly remembered the next line:

"And all went merry as a marriage bell."

The Regent understood her embarrassment and said quickly:

"I can see you are very well read."

"I wish that were true," Zosina replied, "but because I have always had to choose my own literature, I often feel there are enormous gaps in my education, which a real Scholar would find lamentable."

"I think the education we give ourselves, because we want to know, is more important than anything a teacher could suggest."

"That is a very comforting thought," Zosina said, "but to me the real joy is knowing that knowledge is boundless and it would be impossible ever to come to the end of it."

"So you intend to study for the rest of your life?"

"As I am sure you intend to do."

"Why should you think that?"

Zosina paused to find words. Then she said:

"I have a feeling that you are always looking towards the horizon and you know that when you get there you will find there are more horizons further and further still. You remind me somehow of Tennyson's Ulysses, who longed for:

" *'that untravelled world, whose margin fades*
For ever and for ever when I move.' "

As she spoke she was not even certain how or why the words came to her, and yet they were suddenly there in her mind and she spoke without considering whether or not she should say what she thought.

"What you have said is true," the Regent said, after a moment's silence. "But no-one has ever realised it before."

"I am glad I am the first," Zosina said lightly.

Then as her eyes met his, she had the strange feeling that there was so much more that she knew about him, so much that she could see and feel, and it was like opening an exciting new book.

And yet, once opened, it was so familiar that she already knew a good deal of what she would find there.

It suddenly struck her that if she could talk and go on talking to the Regent, he could not only tell her so many things that she longed to know but explain those that puzzled her.

'He is full of wisdom,' she thought to herself.

But she knew it was not only that; it was almost as if they thought along the same lines and she too looked towards the horizon as he was doing.

Then, as she felt that they had so much more to say, she heard the King, on her other side, remark:

"It is time you talked to me again."

"I am sorry, Sire," she said hastily. "I thought you were engaged with Grandmama."

"She has been busy telling me what I should do and not do," the King replied, pulling a grimace.

Zosina wanted to laugh.

Once again he was behaving like a naughty little boy.

As if there was no time to be lost, the King said in a low voice:

"I have worked it all out. When you say goodnight, go to your room, but do not undress."

"What shall I say to my maid?"

"Get rid of her somehow, or else . . ."

He paused and looked down at her gown.

"Perhaps you had better change into something not so elaborate, and certainly without a train. If you are going to dance, somebody might tread on it."

"I will do that."

"Then wait until there is a knock on the door."

"Do I open it?"

"Yes. You will find one of my Aides-de-Camp outside. We can trust him. He is a jolly good chap who would never betray me. I am going to give him a very important position at Court, once I have the authority."

Zosina nodded and the King went on:

"He will bring you to me, and then we will get out of the Palace without anybody being aware that we have left."

"How can we do that?" Zosina enquired.

She remembered the sentries who were posted at every door through which she had entered the Palace so far.

"You will see," the King replied.

131

There was a note of satisfaction in his voice, and Zosina knew he was really quite pleased that she was going with him.

'That will be my only excuse if I get into trouble,' she thought.

It struck her that however plausible the excuse of doing what the King wanted, the Regent would be disappointed if she behaved in a reprehensible manner after all the flattering things he had said to her.

Then she told herself that it would be foolish of her not to do what the King wanted, when so much depended on their being friendly.

'If I refuse him this time, he might never ask me again,' she thought, 'and we would be back to hating each other and fighting.'

She stopped.

'I mean,' she added, 'the King will be hating me.'

At the same time, she had the uncomfortable feeling that what she had thought first was nearer to the truth.

The dinner-party seemed interminable.

When the long-drawn-out meal was finished there were speeches, first by the Prime Minister, welcoming the Queen Mother and Zosina to Dórsia, then one from the Regent, which managed to be both sincere and moving, witty and amusing.

After him the Lord Chancellor droned on for over a quarter-of-an-hour.

As he did so, Zosina was acutely aware that the King was not only fidgeting restlessly in his chair but also signalling to the footmen to fill and refill his glass.

'He is so young, of course he finds this rather boring,' Zosina thought, and at that moment felt immeasurably older than the man who was within a few weeks of being three years older than herself.

There were several other speeches, none of them saying anything that had not been said before, and all of them should certainly have been shorter.

Zosina realised they were all made by people who had to be heard because of their position in the country, and it was with relief that she saw the Queen Mother rise and realised that this would be the last speech of the evening.

There was tremendous applause.

Then in her musical voice, speaking clearly and with a diction that her granddaughters had always admired, the Queen Mother thanked them all for her welcome to Dórsia, and said how impressed she and her granddaughter had been with everything they had seen and all the charming people they had met.

"We are only halfway through this delightful visit," she said, "and I cannot tell you how much I am looking forward, as I know the Princess Zosina is, to all we shall see tomorrow and most of all to our last engagement, in the House of Parliament."

This remark, and the way her grandmother said it, Zosina thought, was a direct reference to the fact that it was there that her engagement to the King would be announced.

She knew by the expression of those listening and the way they looked at her that they too understood what her grandmother had not explicitly said in so many words.

She felt the colour coming into her face and almost instinctively she turned to look at the King.

He was lying back in his chair, quite obviously bored and completely indifferent to what was being said.

In fact, Zosina knew he had missed the point which her grandmother had implied.

She wanted instinctively to nudge him into an awareness that he should show himself pleased and smiling at the prospect of his engagement.

But once again she realised that he would think she was interfering and correcting him, and instead she forced a smile to her lips, as if she, at any rate, was delighted at what lay ahead.

The Queen Mother's speech came to an end with everybody in the room rising to their feet and not only clapping but calling out:

"Bravo! Bravo!"

"Thank God that is over!" the King said as at last the Queen Mother sat down.

He drank what wine remained in his glass, then rose to his feet to show that dinner was at an end.

The top table left the room first, and when they were outside the Banqueting-Hall, the Queen Mother said to the King:

"A delightful party, György! Thank you so much for giving it for me and Zosina. The food was delicious and I enjoyed every moment of it!"

The King did not reply and after a moment the Queen Mother went on:

"I must admit I now feel rather tired, and I think, Zosina, we should retire to bed. We have a great many engagements tomorrow."

They all said good-night, and as Zosina curtseyed to the King, he said, barely moving his lips:

"Be ready!"

She gave him an almost imperceptible nod to show him that she understood.

At the same time, when after saying good-night to her grandmother she retired to her own room, she asked herself if she was being crazy to leave the Palace at midnight.

It was something even Katalin would have never thought of amongst her wildest pranks, and she could imagine that if her mother was to hear about it, she would tell her that it was her duty to refuse the King's exceedingly reprehensible invitation.

And she would instruct her also to inform her grandmother of what he intended to do.

"That is just what he would expect," Zosina argued with her conscience, "and it would antagonise him once and for all, so that I doubt if he would even speak to me again."

She felt nervous and afraid to the point where she longed almost desperately to say that after all she would not go.

Her lady's-maid, who had come with them from Lützelstein, was yawning surreptitiously, and quite obviously she was put out at being kept up so late.

"We keep earlier hours at home, Your Royal Highness," she said as she helped Zosina out of her gown.

"You must be tired, Gisela, and I do understand," Zosina replied. "Now that you have undone my gown, I suggest you slip off to bed. I will manage everything else for myself."

"I'm prepared to do my duty, Your Royal Highness!" the girl said.

"There is no need," Zosina insisted, "and

as it happens, I have to write a letter to Papa so that I can give it to the Ambassador first thing tomorrow morning to go in the Diplomatic-Bag. You may leave, and you know I usually put myself to bed at home."

Gisela was obviously very tired, and with a little more pressing from Zosina she capitulated.

"Very well, Your Royal Highness. I'll do as you suggest," she said at length. "I'm not pretending these late hours don't take their toll of me. I'm not used to them and that's a fact!"

"No, of course not, Gisela. You have been wonderful to have managed the many changes of clothes that I have needed since I have been here. Good-night!"

"Good-night, Your Royal Highness!"

Gisela left the room and Zosina gave a little sigh of relief.

It had been easier than she had expected.

She went to the wardrobe and chose one of her simplest evening-gowns, managing with a little difficulty to fasten it herself.

At home, when Gisela was usually far too busy to waste much time with them, the four sisters always helped one another, and once again Zosina had an overwhelming longing to have Katalin with her.

'How she would enjoy an escapade like this,' she thought, 'and what is more, if

Katalin were here, I am sure she would manage the King far more competently than I can.'

However, she knew that her wishes had not a chance of fulfilment, and once she was ready, she sat down in a rather hard chair to wait.

It seemed to her that time passed very slowly and for a moment she wondered if perhaps the King was playing a joke on her and had no intention of taking her anywhere.

Then she began to wonder what would happen if they were caught and brought back ignominiously to the Palace by the Military.

She would get a severe lecture from the Queen Mother, but worst of all, she would have to face the Regent.

She found herself thinking of the subjects they had discussed at dinner and how interesting they were.

'It would be fun to dance,' Zosina thought. 'At the same time, it would be more fun to sit reading poetry with him and trying to be clever enough to cap his quotations.'

She thought of two books she would like to ask him if he had read and, if so, what he had thought of them.

She was just wondering what his opinion would be on Gustave Flaubert's latest novel, or if he would be shocked by the knowledge that she had even read such a book, when there was a knock on the door.

It made her start, and for a moment she thought perhaps she had imagined it, because it had been so faint.

Then she jumped to her feet, crossed the room, turned the gold handle, and opened the door a few inches.

There was a man standing outside and she recognised him immediately. He was one of the Aides-de-Camp who had accompanied the King when they visited the Guildhall.

She had thought at the time that he was much younger than the others, and he had looked at her in a manner that was not exactly impertinent, she thought, but did not show the respect that was usual amongst those in attendance.

Now, with a grin on his face, he did not speak but merely jerked his head, and Zosina slipped through the door into the passage.

He did not attempt to close it for her but started to walk very quickly ahead, obviously assuming that she would follow him.

She did what was expected, and found by the time they had reached the end of the corridor that she was almost running to keep up with him.

There was no-one about and many of the lights had been extinguished, and she noticed that the Aide-de-Camp kept to the side of the corridor and, where possible, in the shadows.

Then they were in a part of the Palace which Zosina had not seen before and she supposed they were going to the King's Suite.

Instead, the Aide-de-Camp started to descend what was obviously a very secondary staircase.

Down they went, until they were in a narrow, almost dark passageway, and again Zosina found herself hurrying to keep up with the man ahead of her.

On and on, past closed doors behind which Zosina was sure were rooms that were unoccupied.

They descended yet another staircase and this time she was certain they must be below ground-level, until as they reached the bottom of it she realised that they were in the Palace cellars.

There, in the light of two flickering candles, she saw the King waiting for her.

"You have been a hell of a time!" he complained.

"I came as quickly as I could, Sire," the Aide-de-Camp replied. "It's a long way."

"I thought you were going to rat on me," the King said to Zosina.

"No, of course not!"

"Well, put this on and we will be off," he

said, thrusting something into her hand.

She looked at it in surprise, then realised it was a Domino.

She had never actually seen one before, but she and Theone had been interested in pictures of the fêtes which took place in Venice when for a whole week each year the Venetians wore Dominos and masks and moved about the place incognito, enjoying a licence that could not take place except during a Festival.

She saw that the King was already wearing his Domino, though he had not pulled the hood over his head, and the Aide-de-Camp was hurriedly getting into one.

"This is exciting!" she exclaimed. "But please, help me. I am not certain how to wear it."

"It is not difficult!" the King said scornfully, as if he thought she was being very stupid. "And here is your mask. Autal found you one with lace round it, because it is more concealing."

Zosina realised that Autal was the Aide-de-Camp, and she flashed him a glance of gratitude, seeing, as she did so, that, already masked and covered by his Domino, he was quite unrecognisable.

By this time, some of the apprehension she had been feeling began to vanish.

She slipped the mask on and pulled the hood of the Domino over her hair, and as the King did the same, she thought with satisfaction that it would be hard for anyone to suspect his real identity.

"Come on!" the King said impatiently, and now he was walking ahead, with Zosina following and Autal bringing up the rear.

They did not go far, and she was not surprised when they stopped at the cellar door, which the Aide-de-Camp unlocked.

It swung open quietly, as if it had recently been oiled, and now there was a flight of steps.

Zosina picked up the front of her gown with one hand and held out the other to the King.

"Please help me," she begged.

With what she thought was rather bad grace, he took her hand and pulled her rather sharply up the steps until they reached ground-level.

There was a carriage standing in the shadow of a clump of trees.

The King climbed into it without suggesting that Zosina should get in first, and she followed him, sitting beside him on the back seat while the Aide-de-Camp sat opposite.

The horses — there were two of them — started off immediately, and the King, lying back, gave a laugh as he said:

"Now are you still doubtful that I can get out of the Palace without anybody being aware of it?"

"It was very clever of you, Sire, to use the cellar door!" Zosina said.

"There is to be no 'Siring' and all that kow-towing now," the King replied. "My friends call me Gyo, and that is who I am, and don't you forget it!"

"I will . . . try not to," Zosina promised.

"This is Autal," the King said, waving his hand towards the Aide-de-Camp, "and we had better choose a name for you. 'Zosina' is a bit too unusual in Dórsia for it not to be suspect."

"Perhaps you could call me 'Magda.' It is one of my other names," Zosina suggested.

"That will do," the King said ungraciously, "but I think 'Magi' would be less pompous."

Zosina thought it sounded rather common, but at the same time she was not prepared to disagree.

"Very well," she said. "I will answer to 'Magi.' Are we going to meet many people?"

"All my friends," the King answered, "and they will be wondering what the devil has happened to me. I thought those crashing bores would never stop droning on! One thing I promise you, something I shall forbid in the future will be speeches of any sort."

"Quite right," Autal said, "and pass a law that anyone who makes one should be exiled for at least a year!"

"A splendid idea!" the King exclaimed. "And the sooner that is put into operation, the better!"

"You would have to allow them to make speeches in Parliament," Zosina said.

"As long as I do not have to listen to them, they can talk their heads off!" the King replied.

Zosina, however, was not listening to him.

They had left the grounds of the Palace and were now in the open street and she could see crowds of people walking about under the gas-lights which illuminated the most important thoroughfares.

She had somehow expected, because it was so late, that most people would already have gone to bed, but the streets were crowded and she could see that a lot of passersby were wearing fancy costumes and carrying paper streamers on sticks or windmills in their hands.

"It is very festive!" she exclaimed.

"You wait," the King said. "It is far better than this where we are going."

There was a sudden explosion and Zosina started at the noise, before she saw fireworks silhouetted against the darkness of the sky.

144

"How pretty!" she exclaimed, as it looked like a number of falling stars descending towards the ground.

The King did not reply, and she saw to her surprise that the Aide-de-Camp was pouring wine from a bottle which he held in one hand into a glass which he held in the other.

"Autal, you are a genius!" the King exclaimed. "I was just thinking I was beginning to feel thirsty waiting in the cellar for you with everything locked up."

"It will not be long before we can see what is hidden there," Autal replied.

"No, and I bet my damned uncle keeps all the best wines for himself!" the King said. "I know he has a whole lot of Tokay secreted away somewhere!"

"Perhaps he will bring it out to celebrate your twenty-first birthday," the Aide-de-Camp said with a smirk.

"To celebrate?" The King laughed. "You know he will not be doing that, not when it means 'good-night' as far as he is concerned."

"Well, we will drink to his departure," Autal said, "and good riddance, if you ask me."

The King raised his glass.

"Good-bye, Uncle Sándor!" he said. "And here's hoping we will never meet again!"

Again the Aide-de-Camp laughed, and

Zosina told herself it was not the way a King should behave and most certainly not with one of his Aides-de-Camp.

It was obvious that Autal was inciting him to be more rebellious than he was already, and she thought it was a pity that someone older and wiser was not in attendance on the King.

'I suppose,' she thought, 'the Regent thought it would be better for him to have somebody of his own age.'

The King finished his glass of wine, then somewhat ungraciously said to Zosina:

"Do you want a drink?"

"No, thank you," Zosina replied. "I am not thirsty."

The Aide-de-Camp sniggered.

"You do not have to be thirsty to drink," he said. "Come on, Magi, have a sip of mine. It will get you into the spirit of things, and that's the right word for it."

He laughed at his own joke and Zosina found herself stiffening.

How dare he speak to her in such a familiar manner?

Then she told herself that she had to remember they were all incognito and she was not a Princess and the prospective Queen, but Magi, a girl who was fast enough in her behaviour to go out after midnight escorted only by two young men.

Autal had not waited for her reply, but thrust into her hand a glass from which he had already been drinking.

As she felt it was impossible to refuse to do what he wanted and she was afraid that the King would sense her reluctance, she drank a little of the wine, which was quite pleasant but rather heavy.

"That is better!" Autal said as she handed him back the glass.

Then, putting it to his own lips, he appeared to tip it down his throat.

The King finished off what was in his glass.

"We are nearly there," he said, "and one thing is that we will have plenty to drink, if Lakatos has anything to do with it."

"If he is still waiting for us," Autal said.

"He will know I am not going to miss this party," the King said.

As he spoke, Zosina thought for a moment that he slurred his words; then she told herself that she must be mistaken and perhaps he had not swallowed all the wine he had in his mouth.

The carriage came to a standstill and Autal threw the bottle, which was nearly empty, down on the floor.

The King got out of the carriage first and

Zosina saw with a little constriction of her heart that there were huge crowds outside and heard the sound of some very noisy music.

CHAPTER FIVE

The crowds were moving slowly and were obviously in a mood of gaiety and excitement.

The majority of people on the street, Zosina thought, were peasants, who appeared to gape at everything and everybody.

But there were also a number of anonymous figures, wearing Dominos and masks, who were moving in through a huge doorway lit with dozens of electric globes and festooned with bunting and flags.

Because she felt nervous, Zosina moved closer to the King as he elbowed his way through the crowds to the door of what she guessed must be a Beer Hall.

She knew they existed in Lützelstein although she had never actually been in one. She had heard that dances and entertainments often took place in them.

When she got through the door, holding her Domino tightly round her and afraid, because the King was moving so quickly, that she would be left behind, she found herself first in an Entrance-Hall.

There were a great number of people standing about, apparently waiting for new arrivals.

They were very noisy and the Band that was playing inside seemed almost deafening.

Then Zosina heard a cry of:

"Gyo! Gyo! Here you are!"

A moment later several men hurried towards them, holding out their arms towards the King, and when they reached him, they shook his hand effusively and slapped him on the back.

"We'd almost given up waiting for you," they said. "Come on, Gyo! Everyone's here but you."

They started up some stairs and Zosina and Autal followed.

She wondered where they were going and a few seconds later they opened a door off a wide corridor and she realised that they were entering an enormous box.

With a sigh of relief, she knew that she would not have to cope with the crowds on the dance-floor beneath them and would be able to watch without immediately taking part in the dancing.

Then as she saw who was waiting for them she felt her eyes widen in surprise beneath the velvet mask.

A lot of the men had pulled their masks from their faces, letting them hang round their necks, and she could see that they were all young but a very different type from the sort of gentlemen whom she would expect to find in the company of Royalty.

She told herself not to be censorious, but there was something which she thought was rather common and coarse about the men, which made them different from those she had met before.

"Gyo! Gyo!" they cried triumphantly as the King appeared. "We thought you were never coming!"

"Nothing could have prevented me from being here tonight," the King replied.

"Have a drink. Lakatos has brought us some champagne — what do you think of that?"

"I bet you are several bottles ahead of me already," the King exclaimed, "but give me time, and I will catch you up!"

Somebody handed him a glass, which he filled to the brim, and he drank deeply before he said:

"Give Autal a drink, and Magi. She is with me."

He jerked his thumb at Zosina as he spoke, but she was at the moment looking with astonishment at the women, whom she had not noticed at first because they were leaning over the box, waving and shouting to their friends on the dance-floor.

Now, as if they had just realised that the King had arrived, they turned towards him with cries of delight, and she knew that if the men were different, it was impossible to find an adjective to describe the women.

Most of them had removed their masks, if they had ever worn them, and their eyes were heavily mascaraed and in striking contrast to the gold or red of their hair, which was so vivid that Zosina was certain it was dyed.

They all had crimson lips and their faces were powdered and rouged. One or two of them looked like a Dutch doll which had been Katalin's favourite when she was a little girl.

The Dominos they wore were open and beneath them Zosina could see that they wore gowns cut very low; in fact one or two were so revealing that after one glance at their bulging bosoms, she looked away in embarrassment.

"Gyo! You're here! We've been waiting for you."

Their shrill, uncultured voices raved out, all saying the same thing.

Then they were kissing the King and Autal, leaving smears of lipstick on their faces and on their lips.

Zosina stood to one side, feeling as if she

were invisible. Then one of the men, with a bottle of champagne in his hand, said to her:

"Have a drink, Magi. You look far too sober, which is a mistake."

The way he pronounced his words told Zosina that he was definitely the reverse.

But because she thought it better to agree to anything that was suggested, she took a glass from him and held it as he poured the champagne into it.

"Now enjoy yourself," he said. "What do you look like behind that mask?"

He reached out his hand as if to remove it, but Zosina nervously edged away from him.

She thought he would persist in unmasking her, but at that moment the King shouted:

"Hey, Lakatos, I am dying of thirst. Are you out of wine already?"

"You need not be afraid of that, Gyo!" Lakatos replied. "I've enough bottles to float a battleship!"

"We'll need it," one of the blond women, who had her arm round the King's neck, replied. "He's no fun unless he's full to the brim, are you, my pet?"

She kissed the King's cheek as she spoke, but he appeared to be more concerned with having his glass filled than with appreciating her attention.

Because Zosina had no wish for Lakatos to

notice her again, she moved along the side of the box and edged her way to the front of it.

Now she could look down at the dance-floor, which was certainly different from anything she had seen in her life before.

At one end there was a huge Band of what must have been nearly a hundred players. At the other end was a Bar which stretched right across the Hall from one wall to the other.

Behind it, barmaids in national costume were filling china mugs of beer, which were being passed over the heads of those waiting six deep to be served.

On the floor itself, the dancers were either gyrating wildly about or dancing close to each other in a manner which Zosina felt was very improper.

There were also a number of men whom she knew were drunk, because they were staggering about with or without partners and often falling down as they did so.

If the women in the box looked fast and vulgar there were far worse specimens below, and Zosina felt a little tremor of fear in case her grandmother or, worse still, the Regent should know where she was.

At the same time, in a way it was a fascinating spectacle that she had never imagined she would see, and because it was unique she thought she must take in every detail.

As she watched, a voice beside her said:

"Finished your drink? If so, we'll go down and dance."

It was the man called Lakatos who spoke, and she started nervously before she replied:

"I think I had . . . better stay up here with . . . Gyo!"

"You can't do that!" Lakatos replied. "He's already dancing. Come on! That's what you're here for."

He spoke almost roughly, and now Zosina was certain that he had had far too much to drink and she thought that he might make an exhibition of himself as some of the other people were doing.

"I think perhaps . . ." she began.

Before she could finish what she was going to say, he had seized her by the hand and jerked her towards the door of the box, so roughly that she upset most of the champagne she was holding in her other hand.

She wondered wildly to whom she could appeal to save her from what she was sure would be a humiliating performance.

Not only the King had vanished but also Autal, and the only men left in the box were drinking and laughing uproariously over something one of them had said.

There was nothing she could do but allow Lakatos to drag her out into the corridor, having with difficulty put down her almost-empty glass on a table at the back of the box as she passed it.

Then they went down the stairs, Lakatos holding on to the bannister, Zosina noticed.

The noise seemed even worse when they started to mingle with the crowds, and there was also what Zosina thought was an unpleasant smell of beer, cheap perfume, and what she was sure was sweat.

However, once they had taken to the dance-floor, it was impossible to think of anything except how to keep in time with Lakatos.

The Band was now playing a Viennese Waltz and he swung her round, but not in the graceful prescribed fashion that Zosina had learnt with her dancing-teacher, but violently, as if he wished to sweep her off her feet, frequently staggering as he did so.

Only by holding tightly on to his arm could Zosina keep her balance.

They kept bumping into other couples, who shouted at them to look where they were going — an instruction which Lakatos completely ignored.

It was all a very unpleasant experience, and before they had circled even a quarter of the room Zosina was wishing that she had never said she was fond of dancing and had not agreed to come with the King on this wild escapade.

As if to think of him was to conjure him up, the next couple they bumped into was Gyo with the fair-haired woman who had kissed him.

"This is jolly good fun," the King said as he danced beside Lakatos and Zosina, "but it is damned hot!"

"It always is," Lakatos replied, "but there's plenty of champagne to keep you cool."

"You are a sport, Lakatos, I will say that for you!" the King said. "One day I will repay you, make no mistake about that."

"I'll remind you of your promise," Lakatos said.

There was something in the way he spoke, even though he was drunk, which told Zosina that he was making use of the King for his own ends.

It struck her that what might have been just a boyish prank on the King's part, in coming to a place like this with people with whom he should not associate, could have far-reaching repercussions which would affect the country itself.

She had not read history so avidly without knowing that Monarchs always had "hangers-on" who would solicit their favours for personal advantage, and she wondered how many of these drunken and rowdy young men were already scheming what they could get out of the King, once he had complete power.

It was frightening to remember that this would be after his birthday, in two weeks' time.

She could understand why the Regent, who would then have no more authority over him, wished to replace his own influence with that of a wife.

But, Zosina thought helplessly, there would be nothing she could do to prevent the King from preferring friends of this sort to those Courtiers who had always served their Monarch and treated him with the respect they considered was due his position.

The Band began to play a faster tune and the King said to Lakatos:

"Come on! We will race you to the end of the Hall!"

Zosina did not at first realise what he meant, until he started off in a wild gallop towards the Bar at the far end, knocking people out of his way as he and his partner charged directly at them.

To her consternation, Lakatos followed the King's example, and they set off crashing into the dancers while both he and the King shouted and yelled to warn people of their approach.

It was not only difficult for Zosina to move in such a rough manner but it was also extremely painful.

She felt her whole back being bruised by those against whom they cannoned, and her hand, clasped in Lakatos's and held out ahead of them, struck those who were in their way with a force that Zosina was sure would bruise her knuckles.

"Please . . . please . . . you are going too . . . fast!" she managed to say with a gasp.

But Lakatos paid no attention until he reached the King, who by this time was prevented from going any farther by the crowd waiting at the Bar to be served.

"A beer, that's what I want!" the King's partner said. "A beer! I'm thirsty after all that exercise."

"That is what you shall have," the King said. "Come on, Lakatos."

He turned towards the Bar, and as he did so, several of his other friends who had been in the box joined him.

"What are you doing, Gyo?" one of them asked. "There's champagne upstairs."

"Kata wants a beer," the King answered, "and so do I."

"And so do we!" his friends chorussed. "Beer! Beer! And mind we're served first!"

"We will see to that," the King said. "Come

159

on, boys, clear a passage for me!"

They obliged, moving forward on either side of the King and deliberately knocking those who had been waiting out of their path.

Because the onslaught came from behind, most of the men did not realise what was happening until they found themselves pushed over or deliberately knocked down or punched on the back of the head.

It was all happening so quickly that Zosina could only gasp, while the women who had been in the box laughed delightedly and shrieked encouragement.

"Knock 'em down! That's right! Get us what we want! Beer! Beer!"

It was then that the first row of those waiting at the Bar realised that something was happening behind them and turned round.

Zosina saw the expression of one man who was taller than the rest and realised that there was going to be trouble.

He put up his fists and struck one of the King's friends, and his action incited several other men to follow his example.

Before Zosina could realise what was happening, a fight had started that seemed to escalate every second.

Some of the men who were knocked over fell against others, and, not certain who was the aggressor, they struck out at whoever was nearest to them.

Soon there were a large number of men fighting for no apparent reason except that the majority had had too much to drink.

The noise was stupendous, and, to make things worse, Zosina saw one of the King's friends snatch a beer-mug from somebody who had already been served and throw it with all his strength at a long row of bottles that were stacked on the shelves behind the Bar.

There was a resounding crash and the barmaids screamed.

As if it incited other men into a desire for destruction, beer-mugs started to be thrown by a number of those who had not previously taken part in the fight.

A large mirror was cracked across the centre, and the barmaids began to run to the sides of the Bar and away from danger.

As soon as they realised that it was unattended, men climbed over it to snatch at any bottles that had not been broken; one of them, as he did so, received an empty beer-mug in the face, which cut his cheek.

It was all very frightening, and yet because she was surrounded by so many people who were watching or only just becoming involved in the fight, Zosina found it impossible to move.

Then suddenly, as she was trembling with fear as to what might happen next, a man picked her up in his arms.

She gave a terrified gasp and started to struggle before he said:

"It is all right! Keep quiet! I will get you out of this."

She looked up and saw a face covered by a mask, and as she did so, most of the lights in the Beer Hall went out.

There was a sudden shriek from the crowd, which echoed and re-echoed up to the ceiling, but there were still a few lights left, by the aid of which the man carrying Zosina found his way to the side of the dance-floor.

He had only just reached it when above the noise of screaming and shouting there was a report of gunfire.

Shots rang out one after another, and as Zosina started nervously she found herself put down on her feet.

A door was opened and she was pulled into a place of complete darkness.

As the door shut behind the man who carried her, there were several more shots, and she put out her hands to find him close to her.

"What is . . . happening?" she asked, her voice shaking with fear.

She raised her face instinctively as she spoke, because she knew he was so much taller than she was, and he must have been bending towards her, for, without her having any intention of doing so, her mouth touched his.

She stiffened into a sudden stillness, and then before she could move, before she could even finish what she was saying, his arms went round her and his lips made hers captive.

For a moment she was too surprised to feel anything but a sense of shock. Then a streak of lightning seemed to run through her body. It was an indescribable rapture beyond expression and different from anything she had ever imagined she could feel.

It was so wonderful, so rapturous, that she knew that this was what she had always thought a kiss would be like, and yet it was beyond her wildest dreams in its ecstasy and glory.

His arms tightened and it flashed through her mind that if she could die at this moment she would not mind because nothing could ever be so marvellous again.

She felt herself quiver all over, and it was as if the lightning which had run through her whole body had moved into her throat and was held there by a magic that was the enchantment that came not from this world but from the very stars in the sky.

The kiss might have lasted for a few seconds or a few centuries.

Zosina only knew that when the man who held her raised his head, she was bewildered and bemused to the point where, without thinking, without even realising she was speaking, she said:

"I . . . love . . . you!"

Even as she heard her own voice say the words, she knew it was true.

This was love! This was what she wanted! This was what she had prayed she would find, and it had happened when she had least expected it, when she had been afraid to the point where her whole body was trembling.

She was trembling still, but it was now not with fear but with a rapture which made her say again:

"I love you . . . I love you!"

There was no answer, but as he held her very close she felt his heart beating as tumultuously as hers.

Then suddenly she was standing alone and she gave a little cry.

"Do not . . . leave . . . me!"

"Do not move. I have to find a way out."

She stood still because he had told her to, and she knew he was feeling his way through the darkness until a door opened on the other side of what she thought must be a small room.

There was still a pandemonium of noise

coming from the Beer Hall. Then there was a faint light and she could see the Regent's head and shoulders silhouetted against an open door.

He left it and came back to where she was standing.

"We can get out this way."

He put his arm round her shoulders as he spoke, and she felt herself quiver because he was touching her.

He drew her forward and out through the door, and she saw that they were in a narrow passage lit only by one gas-globe.

It was light enough for her to see, however, that the walls were dirty and not gaudily painted like the rest of the Beer Hall.

With his arm round her, the Regent drew her quickly in what she thought must be the opposite direction from which they had entered the Hall.

All the time they were moving, Zosina could hear the noise of screams and shouts and above it all, the bursts of gunfire.

Then there was a door in front of them that was bolted, and the Regent drew back the bolts and they stepped out into the fresh air.

There was no gas-light here but the stars in the sky were bright enough for Zosina to see that they were in a yard where there were piles of refuse, empty bottles, and a huge pile of wooden barrels.

A few more steps and there was an iron gate standing ajar, through which they stepped into a road with apparently a wasteland of shrubs and trees on the other side of it.

The Regent looked to the left as if he was expecting what he saw — a closed carriage. A few seconds later he helped Zosina into it and got in beside her.

It was then, as if she knew there was no need for further pretence, that she pushed her Domino back from her head and pulled off her mask.

She saw that the Regent was doing the same thing, before in a strange voice that she hardly recognised he said:

"Forgive me! I can only beg your forgiveness!"

"For . . . what?"

"For behaving as I did just now," he answered. "You tried me too far, and I can only apologise humbly, and if you wish, on my knees, for losing my head."

"There is . . . no need . . . to apologise," Zosina said shyly.

She realised that he was referring to the fact that he had kissed her, and she knew that as far as she was concerned it was the most wonderful and perfect thing that had ever happened in her whole life.

"But there is!" the Regent said sternly. "I

thought I was a controlled, civilised person, but I find instead I am little better than those brigands who are firing wildly as they always do when they are excited."

"Brigands!" Zosina exclaimed with a little shiver.

"You are quite safe," he said. "They would not hurt you. It is just exuberance that makes them fire off their pistols, especially when there is a fight!"

He spoke in the sensible voice in which he had talked at dinner, and because she felt that he had gone away from her, that he had left her after they had been so close, she turned to him and, trying to see his face in the darkness of the carriage, said:

"I . . . love you!"

"You must not say such things."

"Is it . . . wrong?"

"Very wrong, and I have nobody to blame except myself."

"I know . . . now, I have . . . loved you ever since I first . . . came to Dórsia . . . it seems a very long time ago . . . and I wanted so much to talk to you . . . to listen to you. . . ."

The Regent made a sound that was almost a groan of pain, then he said:

"You must not talk like that. You must not torture me."

"Why? Why?"

"You know the answer," he replied, "and my only excuse is that when I learnt tonight where you had gone, I thought I should go mad with fear and anxiety lest something should happen to you."

"It was . . . very frightening . . . until . . . you came."

"How could you have been so foolish as to let the King take you to such a place?"

"It was the . . . only way I felt I could . . . gain his confidence and . . . trust . . . as you wanted."

"You were thinking of me?"

"I . . . wanted to . . . please you," Zosina said simply.

Although she could not see him clearly, only in fleeting glimpses from the gas-lights on the streets down which they were driving, Zosina knew that he was clenching his fists together.

He did not speak and after a moment she said:

"You . . . kissed me . . . and it was the most wonderful thing that had . . . ever happened to me. Did it mean . . . nothing to you?"

"I am not going to answer that question because I dare not. Oh, my dear, this should never have happened."

"You are . . . sorry that you . . . kissed me?" Zosina persisted.

"Not sorry, but ashamed."

"Of . . . me?"

"No, of course not. Of myself."

"There is . . . no need to . . . be."

"There is every need."

There was silence. Then Zosina said in a small voice he could barely hear:

"Now that I . . . love you . . . must I marry . . . the King?"

"You not only have to marry the King," the Regent answered roughly, "you have to forget me."

"I could . . . never do that . . . never . . . never! It would be . . . impossible. I know now that you are the man who has . . . always been in my . . . dreams . . . the man I thought perhaps . . . one day I would . . . find."

"We have found each other, but it is too late."

"It is . . . not too . . . late. I am not . . . married to the . . . King."

"But you have to marry him."

"Why? When I . . . love you?"

"Because our love can have nothing to do with it."

"*Our* love?" Zosina asked. "Do you . . . love me a little?"

The Regent did not reply and after a moment she said:

"Tell me . . . I have to . . . know."

169

"Of course I love you!" he said as if the words broke from his lips. "How can you expect me to feel anything else when everything about you is perfect?"

He drew in his breath before he went on:

"It is not only your beauty which made my heart beat from the moment I first saw you, but your sweetness, your charm, your clever little brain, and above all because we understand each other."

"That is why I love you!" Zosina cried. "You understand as . . . no-one has ever . . . understood before and as no-one ever . . . will again."

The Regent did not speak and after a moment she said in a voice that trembled:

"I cannot . . . marry the King! You do not . . . know what he was like tonight . . . he drank too much . . . and those friends of his . . ."

"I know, I know!" the Regent interrupted.

"You know he is like that? You know about them?"

"Of course I know."

"He thinks he is deceiving everybody when he goes out of the Palace. . . ."

"I know everywhere he goes and everybody with whom he associates," the Regent replied, "but there is nothing I can do about it, because in two weeks' time he will be free to

170

behave as he likes and with whom he pleases."

"Do you . . . really think I can . . . stop him?" Zosina asked in a whisper.

"Not now that I have seen you," the Regent answered. "I was such a fool, I imagined that you would be a very different type of woman, who would be able to control him and make him do the things he ought to do."

"I would . . . not be able to . . . do that . . ." Zosina began.

"It is no use," the Regent said. "Things have gone too far. The Prime Minister and the Cabinet know why you are here, and so more or less does the whole of Dórsia. Every newspaper has pointed out the advantage such a marriage would be in stabilising the independence of our two countries."

Zosina clasped her hands together.

"I understand . . . everything you are . . . saying," she said, "but . . . I want to . . . marry you."

The Regent put his hands over his eyes.

"Would it be . . . possible if we were just . . . ordinary people? Would you then . . . want to . . . marry me?"

"Do you really need to ask me that question?" the Regent asked. "You know if it were possible and we were ordinary people I would take you up in my arms and carry you away where we could be alone together and I could tell you how much I love you."

His voice was deep and broken and Zosina knew how much he was suffering, and she said very quietly:

"I shall . . . always remember that you . . . said that to me."

"It would be easier for you if you forgot me and everything about me," the Regent said.

"Will you forget me?"

"That is different."

"Not . . . really. I can never . . . forget you, because, in a way it is difficult to put into words, I not only . . . belong to you, I am . . . part of you."

She hesitated a moment before she added:

"Perhaps we can be together in some . . . other incarnation . . . I do not know . . . all I do know is that I have been . . . looking for you all my life."

"As I have been looking for you," the Regent said. "Oh, my darling, why did this have to happen to us?"

He gave a laugh that had no humour in it before he went on:

"I thought my life was so complete with my work for Dórsia. I thought at my age I was past falling in love in the accepted sense of the word. Then when I saw you step out of the train . . ."

He paused.

"What happened?" Zosina asked.

"I felt as if my heart had turned several somersaults, and then you came towards me in a blaze of light."

"Did you . . . really feel like that? I wish I could say the same. All I knew was that when I touched your hand I felt as if you protected me and gave me courage."

"God knows it was what I wanted to do," the Regent said. "And ever since then I have fallen more and more deeply in love, until your face is always in front of my eyes and all I can hear is your voice."

Zosina put out one of her hands and slipped it into his.

"Please . . . will you take me away with you?" she begged. "Could we not go and . . . live in another country where no-one will know us . . . and we can just be . . . together?"

The Regent's fingers closed over hers until they were almost bloodless.

"I could be with you anywhere," he said. "We could reach Heaven. But you know as well as I do that we are both too important to disappear, and Germany would take full advantage of any scandal that might affect the situation."

'He has an answer for everything,' Zosina thought helplessly.

The mere fact that the Regent was touching

her made her thrill, and she felt, because they were so near to each other and because of the things he had said, that her breath was coming more quickly between her lips.

Then through the window of the carriage she saw the lights from the Palace ahead of them, and she said hastily:

"I have to see you alone . . . I have to go on . . . talking to you."

The Regent shook his head.

"There is nothing to talk about, and nothing to say except good-bye!"

"I cannot do it . . . I cannot!"

"I shall go away," the Regent said sadly, "and when you return to Dórsia for your marriage I shall not be here."

Zosina gave a cry that was like that of a wounded animal.

"Where will you . . . go?"

"Anywhere!"

"No . . . I cannot let you . . . you must help me. . . ."

"Do you think I could stay and know that you were married to somebody else?" he asked.

There was a raw note in his voice that told Zosina how much he was suffering.

"But how . . . can . . . I . . . manage without . . . you?"

"You will manage," he said, "because you

are intelligent and because you have an instinct which will always guide you into doing what is right."

"It is not enough!" Zosina said wildly. "It is not enough! I want you . . . and I want to be with you . . . I need your love . . . and I want to give you mine."

They were nearer the Palace now and in the lights from it she saw him shut his eyes as if in agony.

Then he lifted her hand to his lips.

"Good-bye, my love — my only love!" he said very quietly.

The way he spoke made the tears come into Zosina's eyes and she could only feel as if her voice had died in her throat.

The carriage did not stop at the main door but drove round the great building to a side door which Zosina had never seen before.

It stopped and she realised that there were no sentries.

The Regent stepped out of the carriage, drew a key from his pocket, and, having opened the door, waited for Zosina to pass into the Palace in front of him.

Then when they stood inside a small, attractively furnished Hall, he drew her Domino from her shoulders.

"Go straight along the passage in front of you," he directed. "You will find a staircase which will lead you to the first floor and you will know your way from there. We must not be seen together."

Zosina turned to look at him.

There was only one light burning in the Hall and she could see quite clearly the pain in his eyes and the sharp lines on either side of his lips.

They stood looking at each other, and as if she knew there was nothing more she could say, no appeal against what they had to do in the future, she began helplessly to walk away from him, thinking that he was sending her into a darkness that would always deny her the light.

She had almost reached the passage when suddenly in three steps the Regent was behind her.

He turned her round and pulled her into his arms. Then as she felt her heart leap with the wonder of it, he was kissing her, kissing her wildly, passionately, demandingly.

At first his lips hurt hers, and yet even the pain he inflicted on her was a wonder and a glory that made her vibrate to him with a rapture that was almost an exultation.

Then his kisses grew more tender and there was a gentleness that was more compelling, more insistent than she had ever known before.

She felt as if not only her body but her whole spirit and soul were aroused until, as she had said, she became a part of him and they were indivisible.

It was a love that was divine, so spiritual, so perfect that Zosina felt as if God blessed them and had given them to each other.

She knew that love was even mightier and more majestic than she had ever imagined. It was all-enveloping.

There was love in every breath they drew, in every thought in their minds, in every beat of their hearts, just as there was love in the way her whole body quivered because she was close to him.

"I love you! I love you!" she wanted to say.

Yet there was no need, because she knew he was feeling the same, and however much fate must force them apart, they were still one person rather than two.

Then, as if the reality broke under the strain of what they were feeling, the Regent suddenly took his arms from her, and when she would have clung to him, he turned her round and pointed her in the direction of the passage down which she had been facing when he had stopped her from leaving him.

For a moment she could not think what she had to do, because she was pulsating with the celestial feeling that he had awakened in her and it was impossible to come back to life.

Then she heard a door open and close and knew that he had left her.

Alone, but because she loved him doing what he had told her to do, she started to walk slowly down the dark passage towards the staircase.

Chapter Six

The visit to the hospital, which was in a Convent, had been a very moving experience, and as they walked through the quiet, high rooms with the sweet-faced Nuns, Zosina learnt that it had been the Regent's idea that the women who were dedicated to the relief of suffering should actually take their patients into the Convent.

Because she loved him she felt that she was seeing everything in Dórsia in a different way from how she had before, and finding his influence everywhere.

The wildness and irresponsibility of the King had made her realise, as she felt everybody else must do, that it was the Regent who had made the country not only prosperous but well ordered and in fact happy.

There was no need to hear the Mother Superior telling her that due to his foresight, the sick and elderly of Dórsia were better looked after than those of any other country in Europe and that the mortality rate of newborn babies had dropped dramatically.

It was the Regent whose thoughts and care for the people extended over every aspect of their life, and Zosina was sure, without having to ask, that there was little unemployment in Dórsia and modern methods were being introduced into their factories.

Having met the Prime Minister, she was sure that he was a good man politically, but she felt that outside Parliament he was not strong enough personally to have a great impact on the people.

It was the Regent who for the last ten years had done everything, but in the King's name.

It was the Regent too, she told herself, who was trying to ensure the stability of the country when he had gone.

When she looked at what had been achieved, and when she thought what might happen when the King gained control, she wanted to cry out at the injustice of the Monarchical system which put a man on the throne not because he was fit for the position but because it was his right by birth.

But what alternative was there?

The idea of a country where there was no King or Queen to rule over it was unthinkable.

When in Lützelstein she had heard that the

King was wild, Zosina had had no idea what that entailed.

She had never met men who were described as "wild" and her reading had given her only a superficial idea of what any man could be like.

Now as she thought of the way the King had behaved at the Masked Ball, the friends who had treated him so familiarly, and the women who had kissed him, she felt helpless and apprehensive of the horror that being married to such a man might entail.

Last night when she had gone to her room she had been able to think of nothing but the Regent and the ecstasy his kisses had given her.

Because he had swept her into the sky, because he had aroused in her emotions and sensations which she had not known she was capable of feeling, she could not for the moment take in the full impact of knowing that she must lose him.

All she could think of was that she loved him and he loved her, and that in itself was a wonder beyond wonders, a glory beyond words.

When she entered her bedroom she saw a book lying on the table beside her bed and knew then how the Regent had learnt she had left the Palace.

It was the book of poems, written by a Nun, which he had promised to give her.

She was sure that what had happened was that he had forgotten it until he went to bed, and then because he thought she would not be asleep he had sent his servant to give it to Gisela.

Gisela would have said that Her Royal Highness was writing a letter that had to be carried in the Diplomatic-Bag back to Lützelstein the next day.

It would have been then that the Regent's servant, intent on pleasing his master, would have asked Gisela, late though the hour was, to take the book to her mistress.

Zosina knew that although the old maid-servant would have grumbled, she would have done as she was requested, only to find the bedroom empty.

She could imagine all too clearly the panic which must have ensued: Gisela would have sought out the Regent's servant to tell him what she had discovered, and his master, knowing where the King had gone, would have guessed.

Zosina could only hope that the Regent had made Gisela promise to keep silent, and when her maid came to call her the next morning, she learnt that this was what had happened.

"You gave me the shock of my life, Your

182

Royal Highness," Gisela said reproachfully. "Why didn't you tell me you were going out last night?"

"The King invited me to accompany him to a party," Zosina answered. "But please do not tell Her Majesty. She might think it was too late for me."

"His Royal Highness told me to keep my mouth shut," Gisela replied. "But if I was doing my duty, I should report such goings-on when I gets back to Lützelstein."

Because Gisela was really fond of her, Zosina knew that this was an idle threat.

"You have never been a sneak, Gisela," she said, "and as you see, although I was late, I have come to no harm."

As she spoke, she knew it was no thanks to the King that she had not been knocked down or cut by the flying glass.

She wondered if he had worried about her when she disappeared, but she had an uncomfortable feeling that by that time he was already too drunk to remember that he had brought her to the Ball.

It was an inexpressible relief to learn that His Majesty was not to accompany them to the Hospital, though Zosina was certain that even if he had been expected to do so, he would not have felt well enough.

She was, however, not quite sure how a

man would feel after such a riotous night, and she wondered whether, as the King had said that he had left the palace in such a surreptitious way dozens of times, a drunken riot was the inevitable end to his evenings out.

As she thought over what had occurred, it seemed to her incredible that the King and his friends should wish to behave in such an aggressive manner and — there was no doubt about it — deliberately start a fight.

Recalling the sequence of events, she had the feeling that they had all behaved as if in accordance with a prearranged and familiar plan of action.

She remembered reading somewhere that students in Munich were accustomed to rioting in their Beer Halls, and perhaps this was the general behaviour amongst the young men of that age.

If that was true, she was quite sure that their bullying tactics would be greatly resented by the quieter and better-behaved members of the population.

Supposing the people of Dórsia ever learnt that their King was one of the ring-leaders of such a troublesome gang?

The whole thing seemed to Zosina beyond her comprehension, and as she walked round the Convent, smiling at the children, saying the right things to the Nuns, and praising everything she saw, one part of her mind was still preoccupied with and shocked by what had happened last night.

In the last ward there were babies who had just been born and one was an orphan, as it had lost its mother, who was an unmarried woman, at its birth.

"How sad!" Zosina exclaimed when she was told what had happened.

"It is such a lovely baby, too, Your Royal Highness," the Nun said.

As she spoke, she lifted it out of its cot and held it out to Zosina, who took it in her arms.

She looked down at its pretty face and wondered, as it was an orphan, what would happen to it in the future.

"It will be all right," the Nun said, as if she read her thoughts. "We will get it adopted. There are always women who are childless and longing for a baby, or others who, having a large family, do not mind having one more."

"I am glad it will not have to go into an Orphanage," Zosina said.

She remembered that she had once visited one with her mother and thought it a cheerless place which lacked love.

As she held the baby in her arms she suddenly realised that one of her duties as a Queen would be to provide the throne with an heir.

She loved children and she and her sisters had always planned to have large families, but she had always thought that the man who would be the father would be her dream-man, the man whom she would love and who would love her.

Now the idea of having a family with the King as the father was so horrifying that for a moment she could only stare blindly at the child in her arms, knowing that every instinct in her body shrank from the intimacy such an idea conjured up.

She was very innocent and had no idea what actually happened when a man and woman were married, but she knew it would be something very secret between them.

How, she asked herself, could she contemplate anything like that with the King?

Last night when the Regent had kissed her and she felt as if she would be content to die with the happiness he gave her, she had known that anything he did would be sanctified because of their love.

To have his child would be a rapture beyond words. But to have one with any other man, and especially the King, would be a degradation from which she shrank with every nerve in her body.

"I cannot do it . . . I cannot!" she told herself in a panic.

She handed the baby back to the Nun with a look on her face which made the elderly woman say quickly:

"Does Your Royal Highness feel unwell? You look a little pale."

"I am all right, thank you," Zosina replied. "It is very hot today."

"That is true, Your Royal Highness."

The Nun smiled and added:

"I feel this baby has been especially blessed because Your Royal Highness has held it in your arms. As it is a little girl, would it be presumptuous of me to ask if it might bear Your Royal Highness's name?"

"I should be delighted!" Zosina replied.

She gave one more look at the child and wondered if it would ever suffer as she was suffering, if it would ever have to sacrifice everything that was beautiful and perfect in life for the good of a country.

Then, as the Queen Mother was waiting for her, she turned away, feeling as if she left the last tattered remnants of her dreams with the child who was to be named after her.

They had a quiet family luncheon at the Palace, which did not take long, because in the afternoon the Queen Mother was to open the Botanical Gardens, which Zosina had learnt had been laid out by the Regent.

It was a new endeavour for the country and

had brought Dórsia recognition from other countries, not only all over Europe but other parts of the world as well.

Zosina learnt that the Regent had written to each country in turn, asking for contributions in the way of plants and shrubs which would extend the knowledge of horticulture amongst the ordinary people.

"In Britain they have Kew Gardens," Zosina had heard the Regent tell the Queen Mother, "and I was so impressed with what was being grown there and exported to other parts of the world that I thought we would try the same experiment here in Dórsia."

"It was a brilliant idea, Sándor!" the Queen Mother had said. "But then, your ideas are always original and progressive."

It was the kind of flattering remark which the Queen Mother made to everybody, but Zosina knew that she was now speaking with sincerity combined with undeniable admiration.

When they found the Regent waiting for them in one of the Salons before luncheon, Zosina had at first been too shy to look at him.

When she did so, she saw that there were dark lines under his eyes and knew that after she had left him he had been unable to sleep.

He appeared to deliberately avoid speaking to her before they went into the Dining-

Room, but because the King was not present he sat at the top of the table with the Queen Mother on his right and Zosina on his left.

His self-control made him seem at ease, and yet because she was so closely attuned to him, Zosina knew that he was as tense as she was and at the same time aware, despairingly, that time was passing and tomorrow her engagement to the King would be announced in Parliament.

The idea seemed to hang like a dark, menacing cloud over her head and even made the Dining-Room and every other part of the Palace seem less attractive than it had before.

Almost as if she could look into the future, she felt she could see the rooms in the Palace filled with the King's vulgar friends, and see the tasteful decorations changed to the kind of gaudy display that they admired.

And nowhere in the picture could she see herself except as she had felt last night — an outsider, neglected, forgotten, or perhaps, worse still, embroiled in the reprehensible behaviour of the young men and women with whom she had absolutely nothing in common.

"I cannot do this . . . I cannot!" Zosina told herself.

She thought that even to please the Regent and gain his respect she could not go on with this farce, which she knew would be the crucifixion of every ideal she had ever had.

But somehow both she and the Regent behaved at luncheon as if everything was quite ordinary and they were in fact nothing more than the future bride and the uncle of the King.

'Perhaps, as he can act so well, he does not feel what I am feeling,' Zosina thought despairingly.

She looked round unexpectedly to find that the Regent's eyes were on her, and she knew before he could look away that he was suffering as she was and his agony was that of a man who is drowning and has no idea how to save himself.

From that moment, some inner instinct and a desire to help the man she loved made Zosina not try in any way to draw his attention to her own feelings.

She knew without words that his love for her made him want to protect and comfort her, and because she loved him in the same manner, she would not add to his agony but try to alleviate it if possible.

Nevertheless, every beat of her heart, every breath she drew, seemed to be saying over and over again:

"I love you! I love you!"

She almost felt as if the clock on the mantelshelf ticked the same words and the mur-

mur of the voices at the table repeated and repeated them, until Zosina was almost afraid that she herself was saying them aloud.

At last the meal was finished, and she and the Queen Mother put on their bonnets, collected their gloves and sunshades, and went downstairs to where the carriages were waiting.

For the first time the Queen Mother seemed to be aware that there was no sign of the King.

"Is not György coming with us?" she asked the Regent.

"No."

"Why not? It is on our programme that he is to make a speech at the opening of the gardens."

"I know," the Regent replied, "but he has cried off."

"Why do you let him?" the Queen Mother asked sharply. "I should think the people will think it very strange that he should not be there when these gardens, thanks to you, already have a world-wide reputation."

The Regent lowered his voice so that those who were to accompany them could not hear what he said.

"György says that as this is his last day of freedom, he intends to spend it as he wishes."

For a moment the Queen Mother did not

understand. Then she said:

"You mean because the engagement is being announced tomorrow? Most men do not have their stag-party until just before the wedding."

"I told him that," the Regent replied, "but he was adamant that his time is his own until tomorrow morning."

The Queen Mother gave a little shrug of her shoulders.

"Oh well, we must just make do without him, but I shall tell him I think it is very rude not only to me but to you, Sándor."

Zosina could not help thinking that that would not worry the King in the least. If he could be rude or obstructive to his uncle he would be only too pleased.

She could understand that the Queen Mother was perturbed because she thought the foreign representatives who would be present would undoubtedly report the King's absence.

She wondered why the Regent had not forced the King to put in an appearance. Then it struck her that perhaps the excesses of last night were still affecting him and making it impossible for him to come with them to the Botanical Gardens.

Anyway, it was too late to do anything but get into the carriage, and now in the King's absence Zosina sat beside the Queen Mother on the back seat, while the Regent sat opposite them.

The Ladies-in-Waiting and the Court Officials came behind in three carriages, and on the way Zosina learnt that they were to be received not only by those who were concerned with the gardens but also by the Prime Minister and the Ambassadors of every country which had contributed plants and shrubs to it.

She had already seen that the flowers in Dórsia were particularly beautiful, but she was not prepared for what could be done with them when they were cultivated by experts.

The Alpine Section was particularly beautiful, and in the huge glass houses that had been erected for the more exotic plants she saw orchids from the Far East and azaleas from the Himalayas.

Just for one moment did the Regent come to her side when they were in the Orchid House.

She felt a little quiver run through her before he spoke, and she knew as she looked at him that he felt the same.

"You look like a flower yourself," he said in a low voice.

She felt as if time stood still as everything

vanished except him and the expression in his eyes.

It was impossible to reply, impossible to find words to tell him of her love.

She knew, before he turned away to speak conventionally to the wife of a Mayor, that for the passing of one second she had been close to him as if he had held her in his arms.

'We belong . . . we still . . . belong,' she thought, and tried to understand what one of the Horticulturists was telling her, but for all the sense he was making he might have been speaking Hindustani.

The gardens were beautiful and a delight to the senses, but to Zosina they contained only one person — she could see nothing but the Regent, hear nothing but his voice.

As they drove back she thought that the day was nearly over. Tomorrow she would leave Dórsia and perhaps she would never see him again.

The King had said that he would get rid of him as soon as he came of age, and the Regent himself had said that he would not be present at her wedding.

"Where . . . will you be? How shall I . . . find you? How can I . . . live without . . . you?" Zosina wanted to cry, but her training and self-control stopped her.

She curtseyed to him when they reached

the Palace and walked up the stairs behind the Queen Mother without looking back to see if he was watching her.

She thought that either the King or the Regent was bound to be present at the dinner-party that was being given for them by the members of the Order of St. Miklos.

But when she and the Queen Mother descended the stairs again at a quarter-past seven, there was nobody waiting for them in the Hall except a Lady-in-Waiting and the Lord Chamberlain.

"Surely His Majesty is coming with us?" the Queen Mother asked.

"His Majesty sends his regrets, Ma'am, but Prince Vladislav is your host tonight, and His Royal Highness the Regent will meet you at the Prince's house," the Lord Chamberlain explained.

The Queen Mother raised her eye-brows but said nothing, and only when they were driving off in the closed carriage did she say, almost as if she spoke to herself:

"I find His Majesty's behaviour incomprehensible. Prince Vladislav, as I am well aware, is a great landowner and one of the most important noblemen in Dórsia. I only hope he will not be offended that the King is not present on such an important occasion."

"I am sure His Royal Highness will make

His Majesty's excuses very eloquently," the Lord Chamberlain replied.

He was an elderly man who, Zosina had already learnt, had been at the Palace for many years and in attendance on the previous Monarch.

The Queen Mother smiled as if to take the sting out of her words as she said:

"When the Prince Regent retires, you will have your hands full."

The Lord Chamberlain shook his head.

"I too am retiring, Ma'am, as are most of my colleagues."

"Retiring!" the Queen Mother exclaimed. "Is that wise?"

"It is wise from our point of view," the Lord Chamberlain replied, "to leave before we are dismissed."

The Queen Mother looked shocked, but Zosina thought she was actually aware of the King's intention to have his own friends about him.

She could only think once again, in horror, of the chaos they would create everywhere.

The outside of Prince Vladislav's house was almost as magnificent as that of the Palace, but inside it was a conglomeration of good and bad taste, ancient and modern.

It was, however, difficult for Zosina to notice anything, because as they entered the huge Reception-Room, already crowded with guests, she saw the Regent standing beside their host and her heart turned over in her breast.

If he had looked magnificent on other occasions, she thought now that he looked like a mediaeval Knight, wearing the uniform of the Order and a wide blue ribbon across his heart, from which hung the decoration of St. Miklos, which was worn by all the other men in the room.

But none of them was as handsome and outstanding as the Regent.

Zosina only hoped as she walked behind the Queen Mother that she looked like the flower with which he had identified her.

She had taken a great deal of trouble in choosing her gown with this in mind, and it was of a very pale leaf-green tulle decorated with bunches of snowdrops.

The same flowers were arranged in a wreath on her hair instead of the flower tiara she had worn on other occasions.

She looked very young, very innocent, and very pure, but she did not know that to the Regent it was like being struck by a thousand knives to see her eyes looking shyly at him and to know that he could never again hold her in his arms or touch her.

The dinner was superlative, the company

was intelligent and amusing, and the speeches were very short.

Afterwards there was soft music as a background to the conversation, and it was with a sincere feeling of regret that at eleven o'clock the Queen Mother rose to leave.

"Our last evening in Dórsia," Zosina heard her say to the Prince, "has been more enjoyable than any other. I can only thank Your Highness for a most delightful time, and I know my granddaughter has enjoyed it as much as I have."

"It was a great privilege to have you here, Ma'am," the Prince replied, "and may I say that for the Princess I hope this will be the first of many such visits."

"I hope so too, Your Highness," Zosina replied.

She could not help knowing that the King would think the Prince's hospitality dull and boring. She was also sure that he would, as he had tonight, refuse his invitations if it was possible to do so.

Zosina wanted to ask the Regent what she should do in such circumstances.

Should she be strong-minded enough to go without the King, or should she just agree to confine herself to being his wife and associate only with the people who amused him?

It would be intolerable to endure the impertinence and familiarity of the King's friends night after night!

Then she told herself reassuringly that at least he could not have them at the Palace, not all of them, at any rate. That would be too outrageous even for him to contemplate.

Perhaps gradually she could have her own friends, men like Prince Vladislav, who, although he was old, was charming and interesting.

Her whole being cried out at having to make such decisions on her own, and after what the Lord Chamberlain had said tonight, she wondered apprehensively if there would be anybody stable and sensible left in the Palace.

To her relief, when they were escorted to the front door she found that the Regent was accompanying them home.

The Lord Chamberlain therefore changed to another carriage, and as the Regent sat opposite her, Zosina felt that if she was not careful her hands would go out towards him and she would be unable to prevent herself from holding on to him.

"I am frightened!" she wanted to say. "Frightened of tomorrow, of having my engagement to the King announced to the world, of knowing that then there will be no going back, no escape, and when I return to

Dórsia it will be as a bride."

She felt her heart crying out to the Regent with an irrepressible agony, and although he did not look at her but only at the Queen Mother, she knew that he was feeling the same.

There were huge crowds outside the Palace and the Regent said:

"I thought we would not go in by the main entrance, Ma'am, but once we are in the Palace, if you and Her Royal Highness would appear on the balcony, it would give very great pleasure to the people who have been waiting for hours for a glimpse of you."

"Of course we will do that," the Queen Mother replied.

Zosina thought it was a sensible idea that instead of the crowds seeing only their backs walking up the steps to the Palace, they would see them waving and smiling from the balcony on the first floor.

Inevitably her mind told her that the King would never think of greeting the people in that way, then she rebuked herself again for being critical.

They stepped out at the side door which in fact was very impressive and was used on formal occasions for those being entertained in the Throne-Room.

There was a wide passage covered with a

red carpet, and as the Queen Mother walked ahead, followed by Zosina and the Regent, a second carriage drew up to the door.

The Lord Chamberlain and other members of the Prince's party staying at the Palace began to alight.

By this time the Queen Mother had reached the huge painted and gilt doors which led into the Throne-Room itself.

As she did so, there was a sudden loud noise of voices and laughter, followed by several pistol-shots.

It was so unexpected and so startling that the Queen Mother stopped and looked back to the Regent.

"What can have happened, Sándor?" she asked. "Who can be shooting inside the Palace?"

As if the Regent was perturbed, he quickly walked forward and opened one of the Throne-Room doors.

Both the Queen Mother and Zosina followed him to look inside.

What she saw made Zosina draw in her breath.

The gas-lights were lit but not the huge chandeliers which, as in the State Banqueting-Room, hung from the centre of the ceiling.

On the throne sat the King, and at her first

glance Zosina realised that he was very drunk indeed.

His white tunic, open to the waist, was stained with wine, his legs were thrust out in front of him, and seated partly on his knees and partly on the arm of the throne was the same girl who had been with him last night, who was even drunker than he was.

Her skirt was up above her knees and her bodice had fallen from one shoulder to reveal her breast.

On the floor in front of them were the King's friends, and Zosina saw that they were lying on the red velvet cushions from the gilt chairs and stools which stood against the walls.

She recognised most of the men who had been with the King the night before and the same women who had surprised and shocked her with the dyed hair and crimson lips.

Even in her innocence Zosina was aware that the men and women on the velvet cushions were behaving in a grossly immoral manner, the majority of the men having discarded their coats and in some cases their shirts.

She seemed to take in everything in the passing of a second; then the King lifted his hand that was not encircling the woman on his knee, and there was a pistol in it.

He shot at one of the gas-lamps and the

glass from it crashed down on the polished floor, and this shot was followed by two more, while the men who were not too engaged with the women in their arms shouted encouragement.

As another gas-bulb crashed to the ground there was a yell of triumph. It was a sound, Zosina thought, like that of wild animals baying at the moon.

Then sharply the Regent shut the door.

"His Majesty is entertaining his friends privately," he said, but he was unable to repress the anger in his voice.

They went on down the corridor in silence.

The Lord Chamberlain escorted the Queen Mother and Zosina to the Reception-Room on the first floor, footmen opened the huge centre window, and gas-lamps illuminated them as they stepped out onto the balcony.

A great roar of sound like the breaking of waves on a rocky shore went up as the crowds saw them, and hats, flags, and handkerchiefs fluttered in the air as the Queen Mother and Zosina waved.

It would have been an inspiring and exciting sight if Zosina had not felt as if someone had struck her on the head.

By the time she reached her own bedroom she felt physically sick.

All she could think of was the scene in the

Throne-Room. She had had no idea that men and women could look so degraded and so utterly disgusting.

Last night had been bad enough, but tonight, with the King's friends behaving in a manner that she had never before been able to imagine, let alone see, she was disgusted to the point where she herself felt degraded because she had witnessed their behaviour.

She only knew, when at last Gisela had left her and she was alone, that she wanted to hide because she could no longer face the world, or rather the people in it.

"How can he be like that? How can any man, let alone a King, think that sort of behaviour enjoyable?" she asked herself.

The King's puffy face and half-closed eyes, his mouth slack and open, his soiled and crumpled clothes, and the woman on his knee were vividly pictured in her mind and would not be erased.

It seemed as if in that split second of time when the Regent had opened the door, the whole scene had become fixed in her memory so that she would never be able to forget it.

She tried not to think of what she had seen, the women half-naked, the men's bare backs, with overturned bottles of wine rolling about on the floor.

It was all horrible, disgusting, and vulgar,

and she was ashamed.

Ashamed for the King, ashamed that any man could so debase himself when he was the Monarch of a country as beautiful as Dórsia.

Then her own personal involvement was there to frighten her even more than she was already.

"His wife!" she whispered to herself. "Oh, God. How can I be his wife when I loathe and despise him?"

Because there was no answer to the question, she buried her face despairingly in the pillow and felt that even God had deserted her.

All through the night, unable to sleep, Zosina tossed and turned and tried to escape from her thoughts.

No exercise of will-power, she thought now, despairingly, could change the King, and it had been only a child's idea culled from Katalin that anything she could say or do could improve him.

Zosina was in fact so deeply shocked by her first encounter with impropriety that it was impossible for her to think clearly or be certain of anything except the longing to escape.

The hours were ticking by and she told herself that soon it would be the morning of the day when her engagement would be announced to that foul creature whom she had seen sitting on his throne.

After that it would be only a short time before she became his wife and would be competing for his interest, if that was the right word, with the women he obviously preferred, women unashamedly naked, who would debauch the Palace as he was doing.

"What can I do? What can I do?" Zosina asked, and again there was no answer.

Finally, because she could not sleep and felt as if she could not breathe, she walked to the window to pull back the curtains.

It was still very early and the mountains were silhouetted as the first faint glow of dawn rose behind them. There were still stars in the sky.

There were no longer crowds outside the Palace, only a deep quiet while the city slept.

It was then that Zosina felt as if the Palace was closing in on her, the walls crushing her so that like a rat in a trap she was slowly being suffocated by them.

"I must think! I must think!" she told herself.

But her brain seemed a jumble of impressions and nothing was clear except wherever she looked she saw the King's drunken face.

Hardly aware of what she was doing, driven by a wild desire to leave the Palace and the man she loathed, she went to her wardrobe.

The first thing she saw was one of the riding-habits she had brought with her to Dórsia, which she had not had the opportunity of wearing.

She was so used to dressing herself at home without the help of the overworked Gisela that it only took her a short time to put on her habit and find her short summer riding-boots, her hat, and her gloves.

She glanced at the clock and saw it was only a little after four o'clock.

The sky was lightening every moment and the stars were receding until few of them were visible.

Zosina opened the door of her bedroom and went down the passage.

She knew there would be a night-footman on duty in the Hall, just as there would be sentries outside the main doors.

She knew in which direction the stables lay, and rather than ask for a horse to be brought round for her, she intended to choose one for herself.

The side door was heavily bolted, but the key was in the lock and with some difficulty Zosina managed to pull back the bolts.

She found herself in the garden and saw in the distance the roofs of the stables. She walked there quickly.

As she expected, everything was very quiet.

Then as she opened the double doors of the main stable building a young groom appeared, rubbing his knuckles in his eyes and yawning.

When he saw Zosina he stared in surprise and she said:

"I am going riding. Please saddle me a horse."

He was obviously too astonished to speak, but he hurried away and she heard him calling for somebody who she suspected was one of the Head Grooms.

Realising that she had caused a commotion but still intent on riding away from the Palace, she inspected the stalls close to her, and in the third one in which she looked, she found a magnificent black stallion.

It was the finest horse she had ever seen, and she had opened the stable door and was patting him when the young groom came back with an older man.

"Good-morning!" Zosina said before he could speak. "I am the Princess Zosina. I wish to go riding."

"Certainly, Your Royal Highness," the elderly groom replied, "but I think that stallion would be too much for you."

Zosina smiled.

"This is the horse I wish to ride," she said firmly.

"Very good, Your Royal Highness, but any groom I send with you will find it hard to keep up with Samu."

"That is his name?" Zosina asked. "Then your groom must do his best. I am sure Samu will give me a most enjoyable ride."

The old groom looked doubtful but he was too well versed in his duties to argue.

He sent the boy to fetch somebody called Niki and began to saddle Samu quickly and with a deftness which came from long practice.

Zosina went out into the yard.

She wanted to breathe the fresh air, and it was an effort to speak, even to give her orders to the groom.

In a surprisingly short time Samu was brought out to her, and from elsewhere in the yard a groom appeared on another stallion, which was by no means as magnificent or, Zosina was sure, as fast as Samu.

The old groom helped her into the saddle.

"Your Royal Highness will remember," he said, "that Samu is the fastest horse in the stable. He belongs to His Royal Highness the Regent, and he says he has never owned such a horse before in his life."

Zosina thought she might have guessed that the Regent would have found a horse to which she had been drawn instinctively.

She did not reply to the groom, she merely moved forward, aware that Niki, on the other horse, was following her.

She had some idea of the direction in which she wanted to go, and as soon as there was room Niki drew alongside her.

"I'll show Your Royal Highness a good ride!" he said eagerly. "We cross the river, then you'll be in the wild country below the mountains. They tell me it's like the Steppes in Hungary, but I can't believe there's a better place for horses than you'll find here in Dórsia."

The groom led her in the direction he described, and as he chatted on, talking of the rides there were round the city and the horses they had in the stables, Zosina did not listen.

She was back with her own problem, feeling that it was pressing in on her and worrying at her brain like a dog with a bone, so that she could not escape from it, could not force herself to understand anything else that was happening.

In one detached part of her consciousness she was aware of the excellence of Samu and the manner in which he moved obediently to her wishes.

Niki was still talking when they reached the open country, and she felt she could bear it no longer.

She had to think, she had to!

An idea came to her and, without really considering it, she acted.

She drew a lace handkerchief from her pocket and as they were moving at a trot it floated away from her in the wind.

She drew Samu to a standstill.

"My handkerchief!" she said. "I have dropped it!"

"I'll fetch it for Your Royal Highness," Niki said.

Zosina reached out to take the bridle of his horse as he slipped to the ground.

When he started to run back to the handkerchief, lying white against the green of the grass, she spurred Samu forward, taking the groom's horse with her.

She deliberately moved very quickly so that he should think she had lost control, and only when she had broken into a gallop for nearly a quarter-of-a-mile did she release the reins of the other horse.

Then, spurring Samu again, she settled down to ride at an almost incredible speed over the soft grass, which was fragrant with flowers.

She rode until Samu himself slowed the pace, and when she turned to look back, not only were Niki and his horse out of sight but so was the city.

She was in what seemed to be an enchanted land, the mountains peaking high above her and the green valley in which she was riding empty save for the flights of wild birds which rose at her approach.

"At last I can think," Zosina told herself. "At last I can consider what I can do."

She brought Samu down to a trot and tried to make her mind work clearly, as it had been unable to do in the Palace, but the confusion was still there.

The impossibility of marrying a man like the King, and the equal impossibility of refusing to do so, was an unanswerable dilemma.

Round and round, over and over and up and down, it seemed to Zosina that her brain considered every aspect of the situation in which she found herself, but instead of the problem becoming clearer it seemed only to become more involved.

There was the threat of the German Empire, the hope not only of Dórsia retaining her independence but also of her own country, Lützelstein.

She visualised only too well her father's fury as well as her mother's if she should go back home having refused to accept the duty that had been imposed upon her.

Even if she tried to refuse, she had the feeling that her father, or rather her mother, would force her into obeying them.

And apart from that, how could she bear to lose the respect and admiration of the Regent?

He might love her, but he had given his whole life to his country, on behalf of the King, in a manner which she knew now was exceptional and was admired by all other countries which were aware of the progress Dórsia had made.

The British particularly, Zosina knew, would want Dórsia and Lützelstein to remain independent, because Queen Victoria, more than any other Monarch in Europe, had tried to maintain the balance of power.

"How can I fight all those people?" she asked herself.

Once again the picture of the King was in front of her eyes and she could almost see his coarse friends inveigling themselves into positions of power, and in doing so ruining everything that the Regent had built up in the last eight years.

'They must be stopped!' Zosina thought. 'But how?'

She felt as if she were trying to hold back an avalanche with her bare hands but being crushed and smothered in the process.

She rode on and on. Suddenly, after many hours had passed, she found that the sun was high in the sky, it was very hot, and she was thirsty.

She pulled off her riding-coat and laid it on the front of her saddle.

She looked for somewhere to drink and thought if she drew nearer to the mountains there might be a cascade of cool, pure water running down from the snows.

The mere thought of it made her lick her lips, and she turned her horse's head, riding towards the great fir-covered foot of a mountain on whose peak there was still snow.

"It is such a beautiful country," she told herself, "but the man who will rule it is ugly and horrible!"

She felt that if the Regent was with her she would say:

"Every prospect pleases and only man is vile," and he would understand.

Then she was back repeating over and over again:

"I love him! I love him!"

CHAPTER SEVEN

It grew hotter still and she was beginning to think that she would have to try to find her way back to the river which she knew flowed through the valley a long way away.

She was now in the foothills of the mountains and there were huge boulders and also a lot of scattered stones which might have come from an avalanche.

But, although she kept looking, there was no cascade of clear water as she had hoped to see.

She told herself that what she ought to do was return to the Palace, but every instinct in her body fought against facing the problems that awaited her there.

She was still finding it hard to think; she only knew that somehow, somewhere, there must be a solution, and yet if there was one, it escaped her.

"I cannot go . . . back," she whispered beneath her breath.

And yet she was aware that time was passing, and although she had no idea what hour it was, soon the groom she had left behind would report that she had ridden on without him, and she supposed that the Regent would send a search-party.

'He will be . . . angry with me,' she thought, and felt a little tremor of fear go through her.

But even to endure his anger would be better than to be without him and know instead the indifference of the degraded and drunken King whom she hated.

She felt as if her dislike and abhorrence of him, which was very foreign to her whole nature, was degrading her so that she was losing her self-respect and becoming a reflection of him.

"I cannot live such a life, nor can I become like the women he admires."

She was back with the same problems which had beset her all night and had taunted and haunted her so that she had been unable to sleep, and inevitably as she asked herself the same questions over and over again, she could find no answer.

Her lips were so dry and she was so thirsty that her need for water seemed for the moment to sweep away everything else.

And yet she was not certain whether the reason for her thirst was the heat of the sun, the hard riding, or just fear.

Then as she rounded a huge boulder she saw just ahead of her smoke rising on the warm air.

Instinctively she urged Samu forward, thinking that perhaps she would find a party of wood-cutters.

Then as she drew a little nearer to the smoke, she saw a fire and round it were seated a number of gypsies.

It was not difficult for Zosina to recognise who these people were, for there were always a large number of gypsies in Lützelstein and she and her sisters had been interested in the Romany people, Katalin finding them very romantic.

Zosina had at one time tried to learn a little of the gypsies' language but had found it too difficult.

Frau Weber had taught her their history and had pointed out that as they had originally come from India, much of their language was derived from Hindustani.

Moving nearer to the gypsies, Zosina thought of what she had learnt and was sure that as Dórsia marched with Hungary, their customs would be much the same as those of the Hungarian gypsies who were the predominant tribe in Lützelstein.

When she reached the gypsies she saw that they were poorly dressed, but in other ways, with their dark hair and eyes, they were much the same as those she had seen at home.

As she rode up to them they looked at her in astonishment, and she thought too that the men who rose slowly to their feet were nervous.

To put them at their ease, she greeted them in one of the few sentences she had learnt which meant "Good-day."

"*Latcho Ghes!*" she said.

Instantly the gypsies' apprehension was replaced with smiles as they replied: "*Latcho Ghes!*" and a great deal more that she did not understand:

She dismounted from Samu's back and, holding his bridle, went nearer to the fire, saying slowly in Dórsian:

"Would you be kind enough to give me a drink?"

To make it clearer, she mimed the act of drinking, and the gypsies gave a cry to show that they understood; then a woman hurriedly brought a goat-skin bag from which they poured out water into a rough cup made of antelope-horn.

It tasted slightly brackish but Zosina was too thirsty to be particular, and she drank all the cup contained and the woman refilled it.

Then she pointed to Samu, feeling that he must be as thirsty as she was, and again the gypsies understood; one of the older men, whom she thought must be a *Voivode,* or Chief, took Samu by the bridle and led him to where their own horses were tethered by a large gourd from which they could drink.

Zosina stood watching the stallion move away, and then one of the women, speaking a mixture of Dórsian, Hungarian, and Romanian, which Zosina could just understand, offered her food.

She saw then that they were all eating from a great pot of stew which was cooking over the fire.

It smelt delicious and Zosina was certain that she recognised the savoury fragrance of deer or young gazelle and perhaps that of other wild animals which the gypsies could hunt in the mountains.

She accepted the invitation eagerly because she was no longer thirsty but was very hungry.

She had missed her breakfast, and although she had no watch on, she guessed by the height of the sun in the sky that it must be getting on for midday.

A thick stew was ladled onto a wooden plate, and while the gypsies ate with their fingers, mopping up the gravy with a rough brown bread which the peasants ate in every country in that part of the world, for Zosina they produced an ancient silver spoon.

It bore, she noted with a smile of amusement, an elaborate crest which she was certain must have belonged to some nobleman.

She presumed it had been stolen, but she was not prepared to challenge her hosts' possession of it.

She ate what was on her plate, finding it excellent, the meat seasoned with herbs which she was sure had been known to the gypsies for centuries.

She wished fervently that she had persevered with the study of their language, but unfortunately she could communicate only in broken sentences and with a great deal of mime.

Zosina understood that they were travelling East and she presumed they would be leaving Dórsia because it was their nature to wander and never to settle anywhere.

The women were attractive, their huge dark eyes reminding Zosina of their Indian ancestry. The children, small, dark, and full of high spirits, were adorable.

Only the men seemed rough and surly, and she thought they regarded her suspiciously, as if they could not understand why she was alone and not accompanied by grooms or soldiers.

As they looked at her and whispered amongst themselves, she wondered if they suspected that she was trying to trap them in some way.

To set them at their ease she tried to explain that she had ridden from the city and now was about to return home.

She thought she had made them understand, but to show her good will, she lifted one of the gypsy babies onto her lap and let it play with the pearl buttons on the coat of her habit.

One of the gypsy men whispered to the woman who had first invited her to eat with them, and she smiled and nodded. Then he strolled away, still looking at her with what Zosina thought were suspicious eyes.

She was just about to say that she must ride on, when the gypsy woman produced a cup, poured some boiling water into it from a very old kettle, and brought it to her side.

"Tea," she said in Dórsian. "Tea."

Zosina took the cup from her. She remembered reading that the gypsies were famous for their special herb-teas, and when she sipped the tea, she thought the taste was strange but delicious.

However, the herbs were impossible to recognise, because honey had been added, although not enough to destroy the aromatic flavour.

"I wonder what herbs they have used?"

Zosina asked herself.

She thought of the different herbs that were to be found in Dórsia, but it was impossible to translate them into any language which the gypsies were likely to understand.

She realised they were delighted that she was pleased with the tea, and when she had finished her cup they offered her more, but she shook her head.

"I must be leaving," she said.

She looked for Samu, thinking that it suddenly seemed a very long distance to where he was tethered with the gypsies' horses.

In fact, she felt disinclined to move, even to make the effort to rise to her feet.

Then she was aware that all the gypsies were watching her, staring at her in a different manner from the way they had done before.

She wondered why, and the answer seemed to flash into her mind.

Then before she could hold it, before she could formulate the idea it presented, their faces became blurred and receded as Samu had receded into a strange and indistinct distance.

"I must get up! I must go!" Zosina tried to tell herself.

Then to do so was impossible, and she felt herself sinking away into an infinite darkness in which there was no thought. . . .

"Wake up, wake up, Zosina!"

She heard a voice calling her from far away.

"Zosina!"

The call came again, and because she knew who it was, she felt her love rise within her and sweep over her in an indefinable happiness.

"Zosina!"

Now the voice was louder and more compelling, and because she knew who was there, close to her, she smiled and with an effort opened her eyes.

She could see his face, close to hers, and the outline of his head against the light. Then because she was conscious only of an irrepressible happiness, she murmured:

"I love . . . you . . . I love . . . you!"

"My precious, my darling!" the Regent said in a low voice. "I thought I should never find you, but you seem all right. They have not hurt you?"

Because he was speaking to her, because he was so near, she could think of nothing but him and nothing else made sense.

"I love . . . you!" she said again.

Now, as if he could not help himself, she felt his lips on hers, and her heart leapt and she felt as if her whole body was swept toward him by the impetus of her love.

She wanted him to hold her closer and to go on kissing her, but he said in a strangled voice:

"I thought I had lost you! How could you do anything so reckless, so mad, as to ride alone?"

It was then that Zosina remembered, and she said a little incoherently:

"The . . . gypsies! They . . . gave me . . . something to . . . drink . . . I think it was . . . drugged!"

"It was!" the Regent agreed. "And if we had not met them with Samu, we might never have found you."

"Samu?"

It was a question, and he answered:

"They had stolen him, but fortunately I recognised him the moment I saw him with them."

Zosina put her hand up to her forehead in an effort to think.

As she did so, she realised that she was in a cave, lying on a pile of dried grass, and the Regent was beside her on one knee, which was why she had seen his head silhouetted against the light which came from the mouth of the cave.

She looked round her in bewilderment.

On the ground near her was Samu's saddle and bridle, and as if the Regent realised how

224

hard it was for her to clarify her thoughts, he explained:

"The gypsies have admitted to giving you what they call 'sleeping-tea.' They left Samu's saddle and bridle behind, and, hoping it would not be possible to identify him, they then started off on their journey. Luckily we encountered them — otherwise, if they had not led us here to you, my darling, it might have been days before you were discovered."

"I . . . I am . . . sorry," Zosina murmured.

"When the groom returned to the Palace and told me how you had gone on alone, I was frantic," the Regent said. "He thought Samu had bolted with you, but when he described what had happened, I had a feeling that you intended to ride alone."

"He . . . kept talking . . . and I wanted . . . to think."

Her eyes pleaded with him to understand, and when he smiled she felt as if the sun had come out.

"I understand," he said, "but it was wrong of you to take such risks with yourself."

"But . . . you have . . . found me."

"I found you, and I thank God for it," the Regent replied. "And now, if you are strong enough, I will take you home."

"Home?"

For the first time since he had found her,

she saw by the expression in his eyes that all their problems and unhappiness had returned.

"I . . . I cannot go . . . back."

"You have to," he replied. "There is no alternative."

He spoke gently, with a sadness that was far more convincing than any other tone he could have used, and she knew that he spoke the truth. There was no alternative.

As he had said before, the well-being of their countries was more important than individuals' feelings.

"How can I do . . . what you . . . ask me to do?" Zosina whispered, and he knew she was thinking of the King and his outrageous behaviour.

"I will make him behave," the Regent said in a hard voice.

"He will not . . . listen to you."

The Regent's lips tightened and after a moment he said:

"I will think of a way."

He spoke positively, but Zosina knew that whatever he might do or suggest, the King would pay no attention.

Once he was free of restraint, once his uncle was no longer in a position of authority, he would order him not to interfere, and in the circumstances there would be nothing that the Regent could do.

As if he followed the train of her thoughts, Zosina saw an expression of pain in the Regent's eyes, and in that moment she understood as she had not understood before what this meant to him.

He loved his country, he loved his people, and he understood their needs and more than anything else their overwhelming desire to be independent of Germany.

She knew he would give his life willingly in the field of battle for such a cause, but it was harder to live without even fighting a battle on Dórsia's behalf.

And yet in a way, that was exactly what it was — a battle against his instincts, his intelligence, and, most of all, his love.

In that moment Zosina grew up, and she knew that she could not add to the agony he was suffering by complaining or clinging to him.

"We will go back," she said, and now her voice was not hesitating or frightened but courageous.

For one moment they looked at each other, then as if there was no need for words the Regent just raised her hand and kissed it.

Then he rose to his feet and, going to the mouth of the cave, called one of the soldiers who were waiting below to collect Samu's saddle and bridle.

Zosina rose from her bed of dried grass.

She shook out the skirts of her habit, picked up her riding-hat with its gauze veil which lay on the ground, and walked towards the opening of the cave, carrying it in her hand.

When she emerged into the sunlight she gave a little start, for she saw that the gypsies had carried her quite a long way up the mountainside to hide her in a cave where, if the Regent had not awakened her, she might have slept for the rest of the day and into the night.

She still felt muzzy in the head, but there was a touch of wind in the air and as she drew several deep breaths it cleared her brain and she knew how fortunate she was to have been found so quickly.

There were six soldiers with the Regent, and amongst them Samu with his black and shining coat looked very magnificent, especially when his silver bridle was restored to him instead of the one of rough rope which the gypsies had used.

Zosina put on her riding-hat; then, as she saw the girths of Samu's saddle being fastened, she asked:

"Where are the gypsies?"

The Regent smiled.

"When they brought us here, I let them go."

"You let them go?" Zosina asked in surprise.

"To take them back for trial would cause unnecessary talk and speculation," he replied. "We would have had to explain why you left the Palace so early and why, even if Samu had bolted with you, when you had got him under control you did not turn back."

"You are very . . . wise."

"That is what I try to be," the Regent said with a little sigh. "The gypsies were lucky, when I first learnt what they had done to you, that I did not punish them as they deserved.

"Perhaps you should . . . punish me instead. I thought I would never find you. I had no idea that a flower-filled valley amongst the mountains I have loved all my life could seem so menacing."

"I am . . . safe now," Zosina said reassuringly with a little smile.

Then as she spoke she realised that that was not true — she was very unsafe, and perhaps in a more dangerous position than any the gypsies might contrive.

Yet what was the point of saying so?

At least, she thought irrepressibly, she would have the joy of riding with the Regent for the next hour, perhaps longer.

She had no idea how far she had come from the Palace.

As they rode side by side, the soldiers dropping behind so that they were out of ear-shot, Zosina said:

"This is something I have always wanted to do . . . to ride with you."

"There has been so little opportunity to do the things I wanted," the Regent replied. "I have wanted to ride with you, to dance with you, and above all to show you my own house."

Zosina looked at him with a question in her eyes and he explained:

"I have a house of my own, which belonged to my father, and to me it is very lovely, which is why I wished to show it to you and to see you in it."

The expression in his eyes said more than his words, and Zosina asked quickly:

"Where is it?"

"In a valley rather like this," the Regent replied, "with mountains all round it. It is built on the side of a warm lake."

"Warm?" Zosina questioned.

"There are hot springs beneath it," the Regent replied. "I can swim in the winter as well as in the summer."

"How lovely!" Zosina exclaimed. "I would adore to do that."

For a moment their eyes met, and she thought nothing could be more exciting or thrilling than to swim with the Regent in a lake where they would be alone, the blue sky above them, the sun reflected on the water.

They rode for a little while in silence, then Zosina said:

"Perhaps one day I will be . . . able to come to your home."

Even as she spoke, she knew that it was a forlorn hope.

It would be the last place the King would wish to go, and as Queen she could hardly visit the man whom her husband hated and who would, if he had his way, be exiled from the Palace.

As she knew the Regent would be feeling as sad and frustrated as she was, Zosina said quickly:

"I shall . . . dream about your . . . house near the . . . warm lake, and that way I shall feel . . . near to you as I felt just now when you . . . woke me."

"I shall be dreaming too," the Regent said. "At least nobody can take that from us."

"Nobody!" Zosina agreed firmly.

She thought she had ridden a very long way when she had left the Palace, but all too soon she could see the spires and the towers of the city ahead of them.

She looked at the Regent and knew he was thinking, as she was, that now their troubles would begin all over again.

There would be explanations to be made to the Queen Mother and doubtless to all the officials who had been perturbed and surprised by her disappearance.

"Leave everything to me," the Regent said. "Samu bolted, you lost your way, the gypsies befriended you, and they would have shown you the way back if we had not found you first."

"Will the soldiers tell the same story?" Zosina enquired.

"They are my own body-guard from my Regiment," the Regent replied.

There was a note of pride in his voice and Zosina knew she had been right when she thought he would be a good commander in battle and a leader whom any soldier would be proud to follow.

"I am glad that you are protecting the gypsies," she said after a moment.

"I am protecting them," the Regent answered, "because I do not want the people of Dórsia to be frightened of gypsies or to persecute them as has been done in our neighbouring countries."

Zosina, remembering the terrible persecution of the gypsies in Hungary, said quickly:

"I could not . . . bear that."

"That is how I knew you would feel," the Regent said. "I have always worked for peace and comradeship for all our people, and that includes the gypsies."

"As I said . . . before, you are very . . . wise."

While he smiled at the compliment, she knew that they both were thinking that the King would be very unwise.

Already he was antagonising so many people — the Courtiers in the Palace, the owners and workers in the Beer Halls, and in fact anyone who wanted sanity and decorum amongst his people.

'I must try to make him see that it is desirable,' Zosina thought to herself.

But once again she felt helplessly that it would be impossible to convince him that anything was desirable that did not concern his own pleasure.

Because the Palace ahead of them was overpowering, they rode in silence, and the soldiers drew nearer as they entered the streets of the city.

There was only the sound of the horses' hoofs and the jingling of their bridles, and, Zosina thought, the beating of her heart.

She was nervous, apprehensive, and afraid of what lay ahead.

But one thing, she thought, had been worth every difficulty, every question, and every problem she had to face — the fact that once again the Regent had kissed her.

His lips had taken possession of hers and she had known the incredible ecstasy and wonder of being close to him, of knowing they belonged, of feeling that nothing else was of any consequence except the glory of their love.

She wanted to tell him how much he meant to her, how wonderful she thought he was!

But because that was impossible, Zosina just turned her head to look at him, and as his eyes met hers, she knew that he too remembered their kiss.

They entered the Palace grounds by a back drive where there were only two sentries on guard, who came smartly to attention as their party appeared.

Then they were riding between flowering shrubs where the pink and white blossoms from the trees were scattered on the ground in front of them.

It was then, as if the last remnant of the drug that had precluded clear thinking was swept from her mind, that Zosina asked in a very low voice that only the Regent could hear:

"What will . . . happen, now that I have . . . missed the . . . ceremony in Parliament?"

"I imagine it has been postponed," he replied. "Leave everything to me."

"That is what I want to do . . . always," Zosina replied.

But she thought, as he did not reply or turn his head, that he had not heard her.

They dismounted at a side door of the Palace, and as they entered, Zosina had an irrepressible impulse to slip her hand into the Regent's.

She felt that if she could hold on to him, nothing else would matter, even the scolding she anticipated from her grandmother and doubtless the Prime Minister because she had disappeared when she was most wanted.

There was one slight consolation in that the King would not be in the least perturbed.

But she knew now how rude it would seem to the Members of Parliament, and she thought humbly that she must make abject apologies to everybody concerned and never again do anything so wrong and reprehensible.

They walked down a long corridor until they reached the main Hall of the Palace.

An Aide-de-Camp hurried forward to meet them.

"A guard on the roof spotted you in the distance, Sire," he said to the Regent. "The Prime Minister is waiting in the Salon."

As if she knew, without being told, that she could not escape the repercussions of her behaviour, Zosina walked towards the Salon as two flunkeys opened the double doors.

As they entered, she saw the Prime Minister and the Queen Mother at the far end of the room.

Feeling rather like a naughty school-girl, Zosina walked towards them.

Then as the Regent moved beside her, the Prime Minister came to meet them.

Zosina drew in her breath, trying frantically to find words in which to express how sorry she was.

But to her surprise, as they met in the centre of the Salon, the Prime Minister was looking directly at the Regent.

As if he too was surprised, he stopped moving, and Zosina did the same.

"It is with deep regret, Sire," the Prime Minister said in a low voice, "that I bring you bad news."

"Bad news?" the Regent questioned.

There was no doubt, by the way he spoke, that this was not what he had expected.

"We learnt a few hours ago," the Prime Minister went on, "that His Majesty was involved in a riot which took place last night in the centre of the city."

The Regent stiffened but did not speak.

"A piece of flying glass from a bottle or a glass struck His Majesty in the jugular vein," the Prime Minister went on. "It happened apparently very late last night, and when His Majesty's body was discovered this morning, he had bled to death!"

There was a silence in which it seemed that neither the Regent nor Zosina could move or even breathe.

Then the Prime Minister said in a loud voice:

"The King is dead! Long live the King!"

He went down on one knee and kissed the Regent's hand.

Zosina walked across the room to the window, then gave a little cry of sheer delight.

She was looking out on a panorama of high mountains and both they and the valley beneath them were white with snow. The lake on which the huge house was built reflected the steel blue of the winter sky.

From it arose a transparent mist which she had already learnt was the heat rising from the water into the chill of the atmosphere.

It gave a fairy-like quality which made it seem not real but part of the magic which she felt in herself.

Her husband came to her side and she turned to him to say:

"It is lovely . . . even lovelier than you said it would be! Oh, Sándor, is this really true?"

"It is true, my darling," he answered. "Have you forgotten that we are married and you are my wife?"

"How could I . . . forget that? I felt as if the months we had to wait would never pass and perhaps you would . . . forget about me."

He smiled.

"That, you know, is impossible, but I felt the same. I thought that seven months was like seven centuries, but I dared not make it any shorter."

Zosina gave a little laugh.

"As it was, Papa was shocked that it was not the conventional twelve."

The King smiled.

"I was very eloquent on the fact that stability was more important than conventional protocol, and as Parliament in both countries agreed with me, your father was, as you know, overruled."

"You mean . . . Mama was!" Zosina said mischievously. "But that was because she was delighted to be rid of me."

"I cannot believe that."

"It is true," Zosina insisted, "and Katalin said I had grown so pretty, because I was so in love and so happy, that it was more than Mama could bear to have me about the place."

"And why were you so happy?" the King asked in his deep voice.

"You . . . know the answer to that," Zosina said. "It was because I was in love . . . madly, crazily in love with the man I was to marry!"

There was so much passion in her voice that the King put his arms round her and held her close.

Then when she thought he was about to kiss her, he pushed back the hood, edged with white fox, which covered her hair and unfastened her ermine-lined cloak, which was also trimmed with white fox.

She had worn it when they had driven through the streets, filled with cheering crowds, to the railway-station where the King's special train was waiting to carry them on the first part of their journey to his house on the lake.

For the last part there had been a sleigh drawn by two magnificent horses which had travelled over the snow at breathtaking speed and which Zosina said was like being in a chariot of the gods.

Leaning back against silken cushions and covered with fur rugs, she had held tightly on to the King's hand beneath them and felt that everything that had happened since she had arrived in Dórsia had been a dream.

When she had returned to Lützelstein with the Queen Mother, it had been hard to pretend that she was sad that King György was dead.

The manner of his death had been presented to the outside world in a very different fashion from what had actually occurred, and only a very few people knew that the King and his friends had gone from the Palace, drunk and aggressive, deliberately to smash up a Beer Hall where the people were enjoying a quiet evening.

When the Queen Mother and her granddaughter returned to Lützelstein, Zosina was quite content to wait, knowing that her future was suddenly and miraculously golden.

Her sisters Helsa and Theone had asked apprehensively:

"Now that the King is dead, what happens?"

It was, of course, Katalin who knew the answer.

"There will be another King of Dórsia and Zosina will marry him."

She did not miss the radiance in her sister's face, which she could not suppress, or the fact that she was encircled with an aura of happiness that was inescapable.

"You are in love, Zosina!" she said accusingly, as soon as they were alone.

"Yes, Katalin, I am in . . . love!"

"With the man who will be the new King?" Katalin questioned. "Then everything I prophesied will come true. You love him and he loves you, and you will live happily ever after."

"It cannot be quite as . . . easy as . . . that,"

Zosina said, as if she herself could hardly believe that the nightmare was over.

At the same time, she was sure that Katalin was right. She would live happily ever afterwards. It was only a question of waiting.

The newspapers proclaimed the King's death, and, Zosina was certain that at first Germany thought it would be a good opportunity to press Teutonic claims on Dórsia.

Then the speeches from the new King, proclaiming their independence and dedicating himself to the service of Dórsia, were so impressive and meant so much in Lützelstein that the Ambassador looked glum.

"Everything will be all right now, Papa," Zosina said delightedly to her father.

"What are you talking about?" he enquired.

"Sándor will stand up to Germany in a way that György would never have been able to do. We shall be safe, both Lützelstein and Dórsia. Germany will never coerce or force us into the Empire."

"What do you know about such things?" the Arch-Duke asked automatically, as if he felt he must assert his authority over his daughter.

Then he added unexpectedly:

"Perhaps you are right. I always thought that György was too young to be King, and from all your grandmother tells me, Sándor is

241

an excellent chap in every way."

"He is, Papa!" Zosina said.

Then, because she felt she must share her happiness with her father, she put her hands into his and said:

"I am so lucky, Papa. He is everything a King should be, I love him, and I shall try in every possible way to help him."

For a moment the Arch-Duke seemed too surprised to answer, then he said:

"You are a good girl, Zosina. It is a pity you were not a boy; at the same time, I have a feeling I shall be proud of you in the future."

"I want you to be, Papa."

She bent and kissed her father on the cheek; then, hearing her mother's voice outside the door, she moved quickly away from him to the other side of the room.

From the moment Zosina stepped out of the train at Dórsia to find the King waiting for her, she had known that she had come into a special Kingdom of her own which was like reaching Heaven.

Once again, because her father and mother were unable to travel to Dórsia, the Queen Mother accompanied her, and also in the train were Helsa, Theone, and Katalin, the latter in a wild state of excitement from the moment they had left Lützelstein.

242

There was to be one night spent at the Palace before the wedding, and the King had arranged a State Dinner Party.

But this time there were no speeches except the one he made, and it seemed to Zosina as if everything glittered and glistened with happiness as they walked into the candlelit Banqueting-Hall.

The flowers were just as lovely, the candelabra shone on the table, and there was a very gay Band playing Viennese Waltzes in the Musicians' Gallery.

But there was too, she thought, a happiness she had never seen before on everybody's faces, including the older Councillors, who, she learnt, had all been persuaded to stay on.

It was as if they knew that everything would be all right for their country because they had the right King to rule them and he would also have the right Queen at his side.

"Promise me one thing," Katalin said as they went up to bed.

"What is that?" Zosina asked.

"That when you are married, you will find Kings just as handsome and just as charming as Sándor for Helsa, Theone, and of course for me!"

Zosina laughed.

"That may be impossible, but I will try, although you will have to wait a little while."

"Only four years," Katalin said. "Grand-mama was married at sixteen."

"Four years is a long time," Zosina replied, "and Helsa must be married first."

"We will go through the *Almanach de Gotha* as soon as you come back from your honey-moon."

"I may have something more important to do," Zosina teased.

"The family comes first," Katalin objected. "That is, until you have one of your own."

Zosina felt that if Sándor had been there she would have blushed.

But when she was alone she thanked God with all her heart that she was to marry the man she loved and that she was not afraid, miserable, or apprehensive as she had been when she had last slept in the Palace.

The wedding in the big Cathedral had been as beautiful and inspiring as any bride could have wished, and what made it different from any other Royal Marriage was that few Queens had ever braved being married in De-cember.

"You are not going to look very becoming if you have a red nose from the cold," Katalin said, when Sándor had first told Zosina he could wait no longer and was arranging for their wedding to take place before Christmas.

"I do not care what I look like," Zosina replied, "all I want is to be with Sándor. I would marry him in a tempest at sea or in a thunderstorm, as long as I could be his wife."

The snow had made Dórsia more beautiful than it was already and Sándor had said that the huge stoves in every room of the house by the lake would keep them warm whatever the temperature outside.

"Actually the hot springs underground keep the house warm too," he explained, "and you can be prepared to swim even on Christmas Day."

"Mama would be shocked at the thought of my swimming at any time of the year!" Zosina replied.

The King turned her face up to his.

"It is not what your mother says now, it is what I say," he said, "and I want you to swim. I promise I will look after you whether it is winter or summer. Perhaps I should prefer the winter, because I can hold you closer in my arms to keep you warm."

There was a note of passion in his voice which made her heart turn over in her breast, and as she looked into his eyes she knew how much he wanted her, as she wanted him.

Now they were married, they were in the house by the lake, and they were on their honeymoon.

It was Sándor who had planned everything,

the early wedding, the Reception, which did not go on for too long, and the manner in which they could slip away, leaving their guests to enjoy themselves.

They had left the three girls thrilled and excited because Zosina had asked them to act as hostesses in her absence.

"You must keep everybody happy," she said, "so that they do not think it rude of Sándor and me not to be there. But we do want to reach his house by the lake tonight."

"Of course you do!" Katalin said, "so you can be alone and tell each other of your love."

She was speaking dramatically as usual, but Zosina knew it was the truth.

That was what she wanted, to be alone with Sándor, and now that she was, she felt herself thrilling because she was close to him.

Now that she was married, she felt, in some way which she could not quite explain, that he was more masculine, more overwhelming, and more exciting than he had ever seemed before.

"I love . . . you!" she said as he looked down at her, his eyes searching her face.

"And I adore you, my precious!" he said. "I have a great deal to teach you about love, and I think it is a subject about which you are not as knowledgeable as I am."

"But I am a very . . . willing pupil," Zosina whispered.

"You are so sweet — so perfect!"

He kissed her until she looked round in surprise to find that the sun had sunk and it was already dusk.

Later, from the windows of the Dining-Room, which overlooked the lake, Sándor explained how in the summer they could sit on the terrace outside to have their meals and watch the wild birds.

Now in the candlelight they wanted only to look into each other's eyes, and there was really no need for words, because they vibrated to each other in a way which told Zosina that her thoughts were his thoughts.

When dinner was over she thought that Sándor would take her back into the Salon, where she had not yet had time to look at the exquisite paintings on the walls and the furniture which his father had collected and which she had learnt were the envy of Museums all over the world.

Instead, with his arm round her shoulders, he took her up the carved staircase and along the passage which led to their private apartments.

She had already learnt that her room opened into a *Boudoir* which connected with his, but before dinner there had been no time to explore because she was in such a hurry to change her gown and be with him again.

Now he opened the door of the *Boudoir*, and as she stared round her, she gave a little cry of sheer delight.

She saw that it had been decorated with Christmas-trees, silver tinsel, and witch-balls.

It was lit by tiny candles on two Christmas-trees and they blazed bravely like little tongues of fire against the background of green fir. Beneath them were piles of presents done up in silver paper tied with red ribbon.

"It is lovely!" Zosina cried. "You have done this for me?"

"You are my Christmas bride," he said, "and I knew when you saw it you would look as you do now, like a child seeing a fairy-tale coming true."

There was a tenderness in his voice which made her press her cheek against his shoulder. Then he said:

"Tonight, my darling, you are only a child, and not yet a woman, and that is why I want you to think that I am the Prince of your heart, just as you are the Queen of mine."

"That is what I . . . want to be," Zosina said. "Oh, Sándor, this is so lovely . . . so magical that I am afraid I shall . . . wake up and find it is . . . all a dream."

"You will never wake up," he said in his

deep voice. "This is the happy ending we neither of us expected to have, but we should have had more faith. Fairy-stories always end happily."

He pulled Zosina into his arms as he spoke, and kissed her until she felt that the little candles swung round them, and yet their light was in her heart, flickering through her body.

"I love you! I love you!" she wanted to say, but his lips held her captive.

"Can I open my presents?" she asked when she could speak.

"Tomorrow."

"There are so many . . . I wish I had more for you."

"You can give me the one present I want more than anything else in the world."

"What is that?"

"Yourself."

She blushed and hid her face against his shoulder. He kissed her hair and said:

"I love you! God, how much I love you!"

She heard the passion in his voice and saw, as she looked up, that there was fire in his eyes.

For a moment they were both very still. Then he said hoarsely:

"I adore you! I worship you, my lovely one, but I also want you unbearably! I have waited a long time."

"I . . . want you . . . too," Zosina whispered.

He pulled her fiercely against him, then checked himself to say:

"I will be very gentle, my adorable, innocent little bride — but you are mine — mine, as you were meant to be, for ever and eternity."

"I want to be yours. . . . Oh! Sándor . . . love me and make me . . . love you as you want to be . . . loved."

He could barely hear the words but they were said, and with his arms round her he opened the door of the *Boudoir* and drew her into the bedroom.

Here too there were no large candles as there had been when she dressed for dinner, but only tiny Christmas ones on the mantelpiece and on the table, and the light from them made the room, with its huge carved and canopied bed, seem enchanted.

She looked at Sándor, feeling that he was waiting, and he smiled as if he understood and said:

"No lady's-maids tonight, my lovely, precious little wife — just you and I."

He was kissing her again, kissing her as he took the necklace she had worn at dinner from her neck and the diamond stars from her hair, then the large brooch from the front of her bodice.

He undid her gown and as it fell to the ground in a froth of tulle he said:

"You are so beautiful, so perfect. I am afraid I too am dreaming — you are not real."

"I am . . . real!"

It was hard to speak because of the wild excitement that was coarsing through her. It was like little tongues of fire flicking in every part of her body.

Yet because he was looking at her, she felt shy and tried to cover her breasts with her hands. He understood and said:

"My angel — I would not frighten you, but there can be no barriers between us, no shyness, because you are mine and I am yours. Tell me that is true."

Zosina pressed herself against him, crying:

"I . . . am yours . . . all . . . yours!"

The King made a sound of triumph and lifted her up in his arms.

She felt as if he carried her into a very special fairy-land, a land which contained a radiant and unbelievable happiness, where there was no darkness, no fear, but only him.

"I love . . . you!" she whispered as her head fell back on the soft pillows.

Then she thought that he had left her, but a moment later he was beside her, holding her close in his arms, then closer and still closer until they were no longer two people but one.

She was the bride not of a King but of the man whose heart was her heart, whose soul was her soul, and who would rule forever a world which belonged only to them both.

A world of love.

We hope you have enjoyed this Large Print book. Other Thorndike Press or Chivers Press Large Print books are available at your library or directly from the publishers.

For more information about current and up-coming titles, please call or write, without obligation, to:

Thorndike Press
295 Kennedy Memorial Drive
Waterville, ME 04901
Tel. (800) 223-1244
Tel. (800) 223-6121

OR

Chivers Press Limited
Windsor Bridge Road
Bath BA2 3AX
England
Tel. (0225) 335336

All our Large Print titles are designed for easy reading, and all our books are made to last.